THE
MECCA
PLAN

Nelson Lipshutz

ISBN: 061581767X
ISBN 13: 9780615817675
Library of Congress Control Number: 2013940479
Waban Press, Waban, Massachusetts

TABLE OF CONTENTS

For Sallee,
Who is always right

CHAPTER 1

September 5, 11:30 A.M . EDT   New York

David Hirsch generally liked working in the family business during summer vacation, but he hated this part, the sneaky part, the scary part. He walked along Forty-Seventh Street in Manhattan hoping he looked nonchalant. His blue Tattersall plaid short-sleeved sport shirt with the button-down collar, open at the neck, the chino slacks, the worn no-name running shoes, were supposed to scream *"nebbish"* to the passers-by, just as the white paper bag grasped firmly in his left hand was supposed to scream "lunch." The 11:30 crowd was about the same as usual. The sidewalks were dotted with little knots of men with shaggy beards and side curls, wearing black coats, enormous black hats, fringes hanging at their beltlines, and black shoes with white socks. Forty-Seventh Street is the diamond district, and the New York diamond business is a major pillar of the ultra-Orthodox Jewish community. Every morning, they make their way into Manhattan from the Brooklyn neighborhoods that they have, to the extent possible, made into social reproductions of seventeenth century Polish ghettos. Threading their way through the diamond merchants were women from Long Island striding purposefully forward with a predatory, shop-till-you-drop gleam in their eyes; sharp little midtown types off for an early lunch; secretaries carrying cartons full of sandwiches for the bosses who were too busy to go out; and anonymous little men on anonymous little errands. Like him.

David forced himself to look straight ahead, relying on his peripheral vision to keep him posted on what was what on the street. Never look furtive, that was the first rule. Nothing like looking around to show you had a reason to worry. That is, a reason stronger than just being in Manhattan at all. And if you were worried, that told them you were probably carrying something valuable. Unless, of course, they already knew. That was the hitch. No matter how careful you were on the street, nothing would save you if they already knew.

David felt the hair on the back of his neck rise as two big African-American men suddenly loomed up on the sidewalk in front of him, pushing an enormous hand truck loaded with cardboard boxes. He felt his mouth go dry, felt the tightening in his chest as adrenalin flooded his system. Is this the time? he wondered. Is this my turn? Will I just end up in St. Luke's with a broken arm, or will it be worse? Much worse? The two men continued across the sidewalk and out into the street. They started unloading the hand truck, lifting the boxes and shoving them onto the tailgate of the open trailer parked by the curb. They ignored him. David let his breath out slowly and just kept walking. Not this time.

He walked another forty or fifty steps, then turned right into a recessed doorway. He opened the door and passed by the ancient building directory, white plastic letters inserted into a black corrugated felt backing.

David didn't even glance at the directory. He knew where he was going.

The hallway was dimly lit by old frosted glass sconces just below the stucco ceiling, and was permeated by the smell of last winter's steam heat. The cracked grey plaster walls showed their age. He continued down the corridor, his running shoes silent on the worn maroon carpeting, and halted in front of a heavy black metal door with a glass panel in the upper half. The glass had chicken wire embedded in it, was covered by a heavy steel grille, and was bordered with aluminum tape, electrical wires discreetly attached at one corner. The central portion of the glass panel held the words "Hirsch and Sons – Diamond Merchants" lettered in gold.

David pushed the doorbell, an old fashioned brass hemisphere with a black Bakelite button in the center, located next to the door. The bearded old man, standing behind a glass showcase with his eyes looking downward, looked up, saw David, smiled, and reached under the counter. David heard a buzz and a metallic click and pushed the door open. Only when he heard it slam solidly shut behind him did he relax.

He walked in. The walls of the room were painted grey, and were lightly dusted with the grit that coats every surface in the City, no matter how many times it is cleaned. The upper half of the wall behind the showcase was lined with locked glass display cases with sliding glass doors, the shelves filled with an incredible collection of jewelry. The bottom half was covered with wooden jewelry cabinets, thirty inch stacks of two-inch high drawers, each drawer front with a brass pull and a brass frame which held a white cardboard card on which were cryptic notations in blue ballpoint pen.

Illumination came from two rows of simple fluorescent fixtures, a series of naked four foot bulbs beneath aluminum reflectors painted white, which ran the thirty foot length of the room. David waved and said "Hi, Zayde," then walked past the showcase to a doorway at the rear covered with a loose red corduroy curtain, brushed through it, and sat down on a high wooden stool pulled up to a three foot square table covered in black velvet. He put the wrinkled white bag on the table and waited until the old man joined him. His grandfather grunted a greeting, then looked at the paper bag. "So, nu? Let's see what Abramowitz thinks is such great stuff." David picked up the bag, unrolled the top, and turned it upside down over the table. Two hundred carats of unset cut diamonds cascaded across the velvet. "Oi," sighed David's grandfather. He screwed a jeweler's loupe into his eye and got to work.

September 5, 8:00 A.M. IDT   Jerusalem

Colonel Zvi ben-Aryeh sat behind his desk, reading the paper. It was an unusual desk for a military facility, dark wood with an old-fashioned roll top. It had been his father's desk, and he had been permitted to substitute it for the standard issue steel and formica monstrosity because his father had been a distinguished officer himself.

Reading the paper was a morning ritual that the Colonel performed out of a sense of duty, not a desire to relax. You can't make competent military decisions if you don't know their context, if you don't know what is going on in the world. He threw down the newspaper with a snort of disgust. Four wars, God only knew how many skirmishes, and still Israeli existence was like life inside a gun barrel. The lurid pictures stared up at him from the front page: the smoking ruin of the over-turned school bus, the children's shattered bodies, the circle of soldiers with their Uzis pointed menacingly and futilely outward, too late again, always too late. He took off his reading glasses, pulled the chain out from inside his shirt, and flipped open the locket. Too late for my Shoshanah and my Rachel. He looked dully at the picture inside, the beautiful proud face of his wife, the giggling face of his two year old daughter. Twenty years, and it still hurt as much as ever.

He snapped the locket shut, dropped the chain back inside his shirt, and stood up. The Colonel looked every inch a soldier. He was six-feet-one-inch tall. At forty-eight, his black curly hair had a touch of grey at the temples, but it had not yet started to thin. He had a large nose, he was Jewish, after all, but it looked appropriate in his broad face, sitting comfortably between his intense hazel eyes. His mouth was tightly shut. The Colonel did not smile unless he had a reason to. War is a serious business.

Colonel ben-Aryeh walked around his desk, opened his office door, and walked out into the controlled chaos of flashing computer screens and bustling young officers that filled his domain. He looked over the room proudly. So much knowledge, so much power concentrated in one room. The only regrettable thing about it, he thought, was that, officially, it didn't exist. Not that it was any big secret. Everybody who had to know, knew. Our people. And their people, too.

The room was thirty feet square, painted pale green, and windowless. The floor was a mosaic of linoleum tiles, each one in a stainless steel frame. Each tile could be lifted out of its frame whenever it became necessary to access the mare's nest of data and power cables that laced the contents of the room into a seamless whole, almost alive. In the middle of the room were three banks of five computer stations each. Each station had a thirty inch color display screen, a keyboard, a telephone, and a large red panic button.

He walked over to the officer of the watch, Captain Sid Goldman, who was standing by the main status board. He felt a moment's distaste. Another American playing at being an Israeli! Close-cropped blond hair, blue eyes, skinny as a rail. And this one didn't even have the common courtesy to adopt a real Israeli name. Sid. Ha! Committed enough to make *aliyah*, to immigrate, to join the Army, even. But committed enough to stay if the shit ever really hit the fan, when he could run back to New York and work in safety in daddy's business? He doubted it.

"Everything in order, *Captain*?" Sid Goldman didn't fail to notice the sarcasm. What the hell did the arrogant bastard want from him? He couldn't choose where he was born, could he? He had come home to Israel as soon as he was old enough, hadn't he? Some of these *sabras*, native-born Israelis, were more racist than the Nazis! Sid Goldman hoped that none of his emotions had shown on his face. That would give the bastard too much satisfaction. Calmly, he answered "Everything is nominal, Colonel."

Colonel ben-Aryeh glanced at the master status board. All seventeen nuclear bombs in the ready pool were indeed in operative condition. Five were in backup mode, buried and secure. Twelve were on active status, loaded into missiles inside launch silos. Just in case.

September 5, 2:30 P.M. EDT   New York

Dr. Avi Golan, Ambassador of the State of Israel to the United Nations, seventy-five years old but looking sixty, sat in his armless blue plastic seat in the General Assembly, elbows resting on his section of one of the rows of enormous semicircular wooden desks that ran completely around the chamber. The desks were surfaced with green baize that matched the carpeting covering the floor. He looked unseeingly past the placard with the single word "Israel" embossed on the forward facing side, toward the podium on the first raised level of the two-tiered platform at the front of the room where the Palestinian "observer" was addressing the assembled diplomats, and listened impassively to the droning accusations. Even though his Arabic was perfect, he kept his earphones on to hear the simultaneous translation piped in from the glass walled translator's aerie near the ceiling at the rear of the room. That way, he could turn the volume down.

You would think that, after all these years, they would at least come up with some fresh material. Neo-imperialist Zionists, racist oppressors, legitimate rights of the Palestinian people, non-negotiable demands, the same catch phrases repeated over and over, only the order of words changed occasionally for variety's sake. And it all boiled down to the same old message. Kill the Jews.

Dr. Golan looked down at his wrists, poking out of the French cuffs at the end of the too-short sleeves of his tailor-made white broadcloth shirt. He had the sleeves made a little too short on purpose; that way, he could always see the dull blue of the serial numbers tattooed on his left forearm when he was five years old. He had been big for his age, so he had been kept alive to work at the gas chambers, a *Sondercommando*, fitting into spaces no adult could, retrieving teeth with gold fillings. His numbers had been inscribed a little too close to the wrist, a tiny breakdown in the Teutonic efficiency of the camps. But it was just as well. Keeping them always in sight helped him maintain the edge of his anger, even after seventy years.

He pulled his notes out of his silver Halliburton attaché case and waited to be called to speak. The recessed ceiling lights glinted off his bald skull, highlighting the liver spots. His wire-rimmed glasses made him look fragile. He knew it, disliked it, but didn't worry about it too much. He compensated for the fragility of his countenance with the aggressiveness of his wardrobe, all dark navy wool and old school striped ties. He grimaced whenever he thought of the contrast. It was like the joke in the American business schools — dress British, think Yiddish. Perhaps it was not such a bad idea, at that.

From his perch at the desk below the enormous UN seal on the wall above the second raised level of the platform, this month's Chairman of the General Assembly looked sourly down at his agenda, grimaced, then solemnly intoned "The Chair calls upon the representative of the State of Israel." And like runners at the sound of the starter's gun, there they went, the representatives of all the Arab states save Egypt and Jordan, rising as one man, stalking out of the General Assembly chamber in protest. Dr. Golan gingerly got up from his seat, walked to the front of the chamber, then slowly ascended the four steps that led up to the level of the speaker's podium. For the thousandth time, the special part of his mind that governed his public speeches slipped into gear. He bent forward toward the black cylinder of the microphone, its cable trailing out of the back like the tail of a snake, and began his exercise in futility. "Mr. Chairman, the State of Israel calls upon the world community to condemn the latest act of terrorism perpetrated against our children," and so on and so forth, droning on while in the background, his private mind continued its ruminations.

Who are we really talking to? he thought. The Americans, I suppose, nobody else cares, and perhaps not even they, now that the Cold War is over and their President is obsessed with making nice to the Arabs. Maybe we are just speaking for history, engraving electronic hieroglyphs that will be all that is left of us in twenty years. Unless we can come to terms.

And why not? We lived among the Arabs for a thousand years, in relative peace and harmony. Islam despised us, treated us as *dhimmi*, second-class citizens, but it was not our executioner. Our mortal enemy was Christianity. We were slaughtered by Crusaders, not Saracens.

He finished his speech, left the podium, and returned to his seat. It was 3:30 P.M. The Chairman adjourned the meeting until the next morning. A few dead Jewish children did not represent enough of a crisis to keep the Assembly in session any later.

Dr. Golan gathered up his papers, shoveled them into his case, walked to the closest aisle, and continued up the green carpet and out the chamber door. He was surprised to find Hadi Obbaid, the Egyptian delegate, waiting for him outside the door. Obbaid stood there in a crème colored suit, Groton tie perfectly knotted, brown wing-tip shoes highly polished, looking his usual natty and urbane self. But there was a sheen of sweat on the thin salt and pepper moustache that adorned his upper lip. "Dr. Golan," he said quietly, "I have a proposal to make to you. Could we chat for a few minutes in the lounge?" "Why not?" shrugged Golan. They headed down the hall together.

September 5, 11:30 P.M. IDT   Jerusalem

In democracies, even semi-democracies, one politician is much like another. Anyone who thinks the two party system of the United States is fundamentally different from the thirty party system of Israel has never spent any time in Texas, or New York, or Massachusetts for that matter. Politicians in a democracy are schemers and fixers and compromisers and dealers. That's not their weakness. That's their job. Rigid and uncompromising defenders of principle belong in dictatorships.

Prime Minister of Israel Jacob Sorkin liked his job. He even enjoyed dealing with the bearded madmen of the religious parties, the fanatics he always thought of as the "holy nuts." So they were crazy. Who isn't?

Jacob Sorkin has a relaxed, open face, with unremarkable brown eyes and a small, pouty mouth. He was mostly bald, and wore contact lenses in the vain hope that it would make him look younger than his sixty-eight years. He always looked happy. People said he would smile even while you were pulling out his fingernails. It customarily made his face impossible to read, even by his political intimates of thirty years' standing. But as he slowly replaced the scrambler telephone headset on the hook, a thoughtful frown wrinkled his face, a frown in which even the least astute would easily read disbelief mixing increasingly, if unwillingly, with hope.

The Arab League was willing to cut a deal. Not a cheap deal, not an easy deal, but perhaps an acceptable deal nonetheless. The members of the Arab League, all of them, would finally sign a peace treaty and recognize Israel's right to exist. A joint Arab force would drive the Hezbollah, Iran's proxy, out of the Bekaa Valley in southern Lebanon, and Hamas out of Gaza. And the quid pro quo? The Palestinians would get their state, but the Arabs would undertake not to arm them heavily. Israel would withdraw its settlements, all its settlements, from the West Bank, no matter how many protests the settlers staged. Israel would evacuate the Golan Heights. Israel would initiate a program of massive technical aid to the Arab states. And there were to be no limits on the nature of the technical help provided. It would include nuclear technology, biological technology, the whole nine yards.

It was not an attractive deal, but it still represented a stunning reversal of the Arab position. But it was not all that out of keeping with the tenor of the times. Sorkin thought back over Ambassador Golan's report over the secure line. "Look, Jake, I think it's for real. They don't have anywhere else to turn. Oil prices are in the toilet because the Americans are finally telling the caribou to go screw themselves and exploiting their own natural gas and oil reserves. The Americans are also turning off the money to the Islamists who are running Egypt. The

Russians are turning off the gun spigot because they're getting more mileage out of their relationship with the Iranians. The Europeans are dealing with an economic meltdown. And the Arabs know the Japs and the Chinese will just screw them over if they get their hooks in. So who's left? Us.

"And I don't think we have much to lose if we agree. We can't go on the way we are. The Palestinians have already won the propaganda war. The U. S. government won't sell us much more military equipment, even if the U.S. election results in a new administration. And private contributions from the Jewish community are down to a trickle. It's only a matter of time, and not much of it at that, until our lack of money will bleed our military to the point that one of the Islamic states will attack us again. And this time, we will need to use the bomb. When we do, one of two things will happen. Either the Arabs will have the bomb, too, in which case we all die. Or the Arabs won't have the bomb, in which case we survive temporarily only to be strangled by an economic blockade led by the hypocritical Americans as punishment for what we have done.

"If we accept this deal, what is the worst that can happen? We accelerate the Arabs' development slightly. If they attack us, how much worse will it be than if they were slightly less advanced? And if they don't attack us, we'll still hate each other, but maybe we can actually learn to live with each other." He chuckled ironically.. "Married couples do it for decades." Comic relief over, he turned back to the discussion. "It won't solve the Iranian problem, but it will solve a lot."

Jacob Sorkin had to agree, at least from the perspective of global politics. Israel was sliding down a slippery slope. It couldn't survive much longer without peace. But from the viewpoint of domestic politics, this offer was a hand grenade with the pin pulled. It could rip his coalition government to pieces. The "Greater Israel" people would beat the "Peace Now" people over the head, both figuratively and literally. It would be a mess.

But it might lead to real peace for the first time in over sixty years.

September 5, 2:20 P.M. EDT   New York

David Hirsch had taken over the showcase counter while his grandfather worked in the back room. He was not thinking of anything very much when he saw the man and woman standing at the front door. He reached under the counter and buzzed them in. The man was wearing a light blue seersucker suit with a very faint red stripe, and a Panama hat, a real one, with a blue and white striped band. He had a pencil thin moustache, like William Powell in the old "Thin Man" movies. The woman, wearing a pink tank top cut too low and green shorts cut too high, her short black hair framing a face with too heavy red lips and too much eye shadow, clung to his arm like Myrna Loy playing the Thin Man's wife. David walked over to help them, his face open and friendly. David was a fan of old movies. He had liked "The Thin Man."

The Panama hat reached slowly into his jacket pocket and extracted a small canvas drawstring bag. "I just inherited these from my mother, sir," he said, "and I need an appraisal for the taxes. Could you take a look at them, please? And let me know whether I ought to hang onto them or sell them?" He smiled ingratiatingly.

David smiled back and took the bag. Keeping the bag in sight, he loosened the drawstring and spilled the contents out onto the table. The bag contained three small brilliant-cut stones, about a carat each. David reached into his pocket, took out an eye loupe, and looked at the stones. It took only a minute. Poor guy, he thought, he thinks he's got a fortune here, and all he has are three second-rate zircons. The whole works is worth seventy-five bucks, tops. He put the stones down, bent over a little to drop the eye loupe out into his hands, and straightened up to find himself looking down the barrel of a revolver. David had never seen a real gun up close. To him, the cheap little .22 looked like a cannon.

"Those weren't so great, huh?" Panama hat was still smiling. "Well, I think that you have some stones here that are a whole lot better. So why don't we replace the ones I gave you with some better ones?" He gestured toward the back room with the revolver. David stayed behind the counter as he started walking toward the back room, while the gunman and his lady friend walked along in parallel in front of it. Oh God, thought David, I don't want Zayde to get hurt!

David reached out to move the door curtain aside. As he touched the curtain, he suddenly found himself flung sideways by a firm shove to his chest. He spun around as his back slammed into the edge of the cabinets behind the counter, to see the robbers staring unbelievingly at the doorway to the back room. He followed their gaze to see his grandfather calmly holding a double barreled shotgun trained on the robbers. David could see that both hammers were cocked.

"Alright, big shot, what are you gonna do now? Shoot me?" David heard his grandfather saying. "Bad idea! When the bullet hits me, it will hurt like crazy, so I'll squeeze the trigger, and with this *shpritzer*, this spray gun, I can't miss. I die, but you die too. So don't shoot. I have a better idea. The door isn't locked from the inside. Why don't you and the lady just go away? That's a good idea, yeah? Go on, shoo!" David's grandfather gestured toward the door with the barrels. The man with the moustache and his girlfriend didn't need a second invitation. They were out the door, down the corridor, and out on the street before David was fully aware of what had happened.

David watched his grandfather gently uncock the hammers, then break open the breech and extract the two double-ought shot shells, their brass bases and red plastic cases looking incongruous in his delicate jeweler's hands. His grandfather dropped the shells into his pocket, then leaned the shotgun in a corner behind the curtain and came back into the store. He looked satisfied. He picked up the telephone and called the police.

The detectives arrived in fifteen minutes, right out of central casting. The old fat bald one was wearing a rumpled brown suit and a flowered tie. The young thin one needed a shave and was wearing a tan sport coat he thought made him look like Don Johnson in "Miami Vice." They both looked bored. They wrote down descriptions of the two bandits in their little spiral notebooks, and asked David and his grandfather to come down to police headquarters in the morning to look at mug shots. The only flicker of interest in their eyes arose when they saw the shotgun, but it faded when David's grandfather produced a valid firearms license.

When the detectives had left, David's grandfather called him into the back room, pulled a red pottery cup with cracked glazing out of a wooden cabinet, and poured him a cup of coffee from an ancient aluminum coffee maker sitting on a rickety table in the corner. He looked at David appraisingly. "You don't look so good, *boychik*. What's the problem?" David slurped the coffee noisily, looking down at the floor. He was embarrassed. But he finally answered, "Zayde, I'm ashamed to admit it, but I was scared. And I was also shocked. I never imagined you holding a gun. It's not...not... not *Jewish*!" He blushed.

David's grandfather gave him a long, slow look. Then he sat him down at the table with diamonds still carelessly strewn across it, and perched easily on a high stool across from him. He waited for David to raise his eyes. "*Boychik*," he said, "let me teach you something you're not going to learn in that college if you stay there a hundred years. I used to agree with you. When the Germans came for me and my family in Riga in 1941, we didn't have a gun because almost everybody agreed with you that it wasn't Jewish. Even in the camps, when they raped and murdered my mother and my sister while I watched, I agreed with you." Tears started in David's grandfather's eyes and rolled down his cheeks. But the old man's voice kept on steadily. "I said to myself `These people are animals, this is not the way it will always be, we Jews cannot become like them.' When I was liberated, all thirty-seven pounds of seven-year-old me, lice-ridden, covered with sores, I still agreed with you, because I knew I was coming to America, the *goldene Medina*, the Golden Land, and I knew that here there would be no animals." He sighed and repeated the words. "No animals." Then his face got hard in a way that David had never seen before. A glint of fury shone in the pupils as he continued, "But I'll tell you something funny, *boychik*. When I got off the boat in 1946 in New York, do you know what the first thing I heard was? It was a bunch of longshoremen shouting at me. My English was non-existent, so I asked your great-aunt Sadie what they were saying. And she got a look on her face that told me all I needed to know. She hurried me along the pier past the drunken mob of them, her arm around my waist, while they laughed and jeered and hooted. Even in America, I thought, even after everything, they still want us all dead.

"But America is a wonderful country, *boychik*. You know why? Because you can stand up for yourself! So as soon as I was old enough and I had two nickels to rub together, I bought that shotgun. I looked in the telephone book and I found a man who would teach me how to use it. And I got a permit to keep it in the store. When I had some more money together, I got some more guns, and I kept them at home in a safe. I never had to shoot them at anybody. But I did have to show them a few times, like today. And you know something? When they know you're not going to just lie down and take it, they run away!"

David's grandfather stood, picked the shotgun up and sighted down the barrels. "David, I'll tell you something," he said. "A Jew without a gun is a suicidal idiot."

CHAPTER 2

September 10, 7:00 P.M . IDT   Jerusalem

C olonel ben-Aryeh, sweating in the early evening heat, shouldered his way aggressively through the crowd in front of the King David Hotel. The armpits of his white shirt were soaked. He was out of uniform tonight, he thought, that was the trouble. You'd think that Israelis had worse manners than cattle, with the pushing and crowding and yelling that seemed to go on everywhere. And yet, people were always considerate of you when they knew you were in the Army. Israel was a funny place.

He just managed to avoid getting hit in the eye by the corner of a placard. The placards were in English, of course, since they were directed to the foreign tourists who were the only ones who could afford to stay at the King David, and to the American television cameras that followed the tourists around, hoping for a terrorist incident but willing to settle for a little political discord. Ordinarily, Colonel ben-Aryeh would have hung around to listen to the inevitable arguments among the demonstrators. But tonight he had something better to do. Much better.

He walked across the lobby and into the Oriental bar and there she was, sitting demurely at a table, waiting for him. The white linen of her dress contrasted sharply with her deeply tanned face and neck and the tight coil of black hair pinned on top of her head. She sat forward on the edge of her seat, her bare legs drawn slightly under her with the left crossed behind the right. Her right arm rested on the glass table top, delicate fingers holding the straw rising out of her drink as she sipped it. She looked up and saw him, and her face broke into a broad smile. He slipped into the chair beside her, leaned over to give her a kiss, then leaned back and looked at her and thought how lucky he was to have found some-one like this again.

"So, Zvi, any news from the front? Or the back, or wherever it is that you work?" She wrinkled her nose at him. It was not so easy for a newspaper reporter to spend time with a man who would not, could not, tell her any-thing about his job. But she knew better than to press him too hard. In Israel, everybody knows that there are some things you don't want to know.

"Nothing new, Hannah, everything just the same, as always," he replied, and turned to try to catch the eye of a passing waiter, no mean feat. Hannah sighed. "Sure, sure, and even if there were, you couldn't tell me anyway. So let's talk about something else. Like those *meshuganehs*, those crazies, out on the hot sidewalk." She glanced through the lobby door at the crowd surg-ing back and forth as groups of hardline religious party hecklers shouted at the main body with their "Peace Now" signs. Her lovely face grew pensive. "For them, it's easy. They *know* the truth. They're all true believers, one way or the other. I only wish I knew what to believe. And whom to trust. It would be so good to live in peace for a while. But not by being dead." She shuddered.

"Hannah, my darling, I can help you out a little with that question. You can believe that I love you very, very much, and that if we go over to your apartment, I will show you just how much." He raised his eyebrows at her, saying "trust me." Hannah laughed. Zvi threw some money on the table and they strolled out of the bar.

September 10, 12:05 P.M. EDT New York

David bounced from side to side in the passenger seat of the old Pontiac as his grandfather drove confidently through the woods down the rutted gravel road. Only an hour and a half out of the city on a beautiful afternoon, and he felt like Daniel Boone. A chaotic mix of old oaks, young maples, and a bunch of trees David couldn't even recognize pressed in toward them, arching so far over that they blocked out the sun, leaving the road in perpetual twilight. This is not the place for a nice Jewish boy, he thought to himself.

The road turned right and suddenly opened out into a wide gravel lot in which a dozen other vehicles, mostly jeeps, campers, and pickup trucks, were already parked. David's grandfather pulled up next to a mud-spattered Ford Explorer topped with off-road spotlights, and the Pontiac coughed to a halt. They got out of the car and walked back to the trunk. David's grandfather opened it and pointed to a large camouflage pattern canvas duffel bag. "*Schlepp* that bag out of there, *boychik*!" he ordered cheerily. David reached in, grasped the webbing handles, and lifted the bag out of the trunk. It was heavy. David's grandfather slammed the trunk shut, then the two of them walked across the lot to a large rustic building with a single door and no windows. His grandfather opened the door, impatiently waved David through, then closed the door behind them.

David looked around with mounting discomfort. The split log walls were covered with posters and lists of names, apparently for some kind of competition. A cheap Walmart panel television hung on the wall in one corner, and next to it was a vinyl-covered metal shelf filled with trophies. One end of the room terminated in a blank wall with a heavy door containing a tiny reinforced window, above which hung a black plastic sign with the word "RANGE" cut into it in white letters. From behind the door came a steady but irregular stream of muffled pops. A smoky smell hung in the air. The rest of the room was filled with folding picnic tables, bedraggled metal folding chairs, and a few old padded armchairs, their cracking vinyl allowing horsehair tufts to poke through. Sprawled about on the chairs were ten or twelve men in peaked caps, plaid shirts, jeans and heavy work shoes, looking incuriously at them. David started to squirm. It was what he imagined a meeting of the KKK would be like.

None of this seemed to bother his grandfather at all. He pointed to one of the tables, and David swung the bag up onto it. His grandfather unzipped the bag and proceeded to pull out a stainless steel Smith and Wesson Model 66 revolver, a worn Army-issue .45 semi-automatic pistol, several boxes of cartridges, and two pairs of large plastic earmuffs. As he looked over the gear, a large man wearing a red baseball cap with the words "Range Safety Officer" in blue block letters on the front, heaved himself out of one of the armchairs and walked over to them. Over a checked flannel shirt, he wore a dark green shooting vest with multiple pockets. Every flat space bore an ornamental patch, most with pictures of guns on them. His heavy hands, rough and calloused, were hooked into the tops of the pockets of his worn jeans. He needed a shave. "Hi, Izzie," he said. "Who's the kid?" My God, thought David, Zayde *knows* these people. "Hello, Fred," his grandfather replied. "This is my grandson David. It's time the boy learned to shoot, so you're going to see us here a lot for a while. You're gonna see us on the indoor range, on the rifle range, shooting my shotgun on the trap range. David," he continued, "say hello to Fred Markowitz." The huge man extended his hand. David grasped it dazedly. Markowitz? *Markowitz*? What kind of name was that for somebody in the KKK? David had the feeling that this was going to be a very educational afternoon.

September 10, 11:42 P.M. IDT Jerusalem

Jacob Sorkin sat in the middle of the long rosewood table and listened to the shouting. If two Jews have three opinions, he wondered idly, how many opinions do thirty Jews have? Too many opinions, that was for sure. This wasn't going to get anywhere. He'd rather have consensus. But he'd have to settle for victory.

He leaned forward and banged on the table with his fist, making the water glasses rattle. "*Shah*! Quiet! We have been going around in circles on this for the past fifteen hours. That's enough talk! It's already almost midnight. Now I'm going to tell you what I'm going to do. I am going to appoint a delegation to sit down with the Arab League and begin to draft a treaty embodying their proposal. I don't trust them any more than any person around this table does. But we can't say no to this offer. We may never get another chance to say yes." He looked around the table coldly. "And I will *never* forget anybody who crosses me on this one, believe me. *Never.*"

"So you'll never forget. Neither does an elephant. So what?" Eliyahu Bender, who had his Cabinet seat by virtue of a deal with his ultra-Orthodox splinter party that made even Jacob Sorkin uncomfortable, shrugged his disdain, his big shoulders hunching under the black coat he wore even in the summer, his shaggy beard jumping as he spoke. "You're giving back Judaea and Samaria? Not with my help, you're not! I'll vote with the *goyim*, the non-Jews, before I'll stand still for that! Nobody gives back one square inch of *Eretz Yisroel*! God gave it to us, and it's ours! Period, the end! We vote `no confidence' tomorrow, and you can go spend your time sleeping in the park while we put together a new government — without you!" He reached up and resettled his broad-brimmed round black hat more firmly on his head. He flashed Sorkin a final dirty look.

Jacob Sorkin liked Eliyahu Bender, especially when Eliyahu was giving him hell. Agree with him or not, you certainly always knew where he stood. And he appreciated Eliyahu's need to make his record, to be able to say he took his stand. But it was really all over. He had to wind things up, even if he had to hurt Eliyahu's feelings a bit. Sorkin looked ironically down the table. "No you won't, my friend, no you won't. I'm only a politician, but I can count. I've got the votes. Not by much, but by enough. We're going to try it my way." The meeting broke up noisily. I just can't wait to see the papers tomorrow morning, thought Sorkin dismally as he walked briskly down the hall and up two flights of steps to his office.

He sat down behind his immense wooden desk and gently swiveled back and forth, his gaze drifting over the signed photographs covering the walls. Sorkin was catholic in his taste. He had pictures with Ariel Sharon, Benyamin Netanyahu, Menachem Begin, with everybody, regardless of party, regardless of philosophy, just as long as they had the good of Israel in their hearts. How will they think of me in a hundred years? he wondered. As a wise one, or as a fool. Or worse, as a traitor.

He looked out through the window over the hills of the city. The sight still moved him every time. Thousands of years, and Jerusalem is still here. And we're still here, or here again, it really doesn't matter. So long as we stay here. And we won't stay here without peace. I just hope we stay here making peace this way.

He heard a knock at the door. He called out "Come in," and was surprised to see Eliyahu Bender trot into the room. Bender plopped down in the upholstered chair in front of the desk, and said "Nu, Jake, aren't you going to offer a poor religious nut something to keep the chill off?" Sorkin grunted, spun his chair to the right, reached into a drawer and pulled out an almost full bottle of Slivovitz, the plum brandy that he had drunk since he was a boy in Lithuania, in another life, it seemed. He took out two shot glasses, filled them, handed one to Bender and kept one for himself. He lifted his glass, said "*L'chaim*, to life!" and drained it. Bender did the same, then thumped his chest with the side of his fist and exhaled appreciatively. He put the shot glass down and looked Sorkin straight in the eye. Sorkin waited patiently. He had learned some very important things over the years at times like this, late at night over a glass of Slivovitz.

"So why am I here?" Bender started out. "Not to lobby you, don't worry. I know you've made your decision. And maybe it's the right one, who knows, although I'll deny under oath that I ever said that, so don't get any funny ideas." Bender looked at him sharply. Sorkin nodded. It was OK. Bender continued, "Look, Jake, when you sit down this time it's not going to be just with the Egyptians or the Saudis or the Jordanians. It's going to be with all of them. And there are some very different concepts of honesty floating around out there in the world of Islam. You don't know too much about religion, you *goy*." His smile made it alright. "How much do you know about *Shi'a*?" Sorkin didn't see where this was going, but he played along. "Not much," he answered. "It's just a peculiar sect of Islam, like Reform for us." Bender shook his head. "No, it's not like Reform. Look, the thing you have to understand, Jake, is that *Shi'a*, what the Shiites who run Iraq and Syria and have a lot of influence everywhere else believe, was viewed as a heresy for hundreds of years, and the Shiites were persecuted brutally. Now what does persecution always call forth? One thing, Jake, always one thing: *secrecy*. For an organization like the Mafia in Sicily, which started out as a political resistance movement against their French overlords, it meant the code of *omerta*, silence. Tell the oppressor nothing. For the Shiites, it developed into something else. Ever hear of *taqiyah*?" Sorkin shook his head. Bender continued "Well, it's time you did. *Taqiyah* is *omerta* with bells on. The Shiites made it a moral imperative to deny they were Shiites to anybody outside the sect. It was a sin to disclose your true beliefs to an outsider, even if that meant you denied your most deeply held beliefs publically in the face of the world. And the idea got adopted by the

Sunnis, too. The very concept of honesty when dealing with infidels is heresy. I know you don't trust them, but this goes beyond normal dishonesty. They are under an absolute obligation to lie. For these people, lying is not a sin —it's a holy act. So watch yourself, Jake, watch yourself very carefully." Bender stood up and headed for the door. "And thanks for the Slivovitz." Jacob Sorkin watched him go out the door. Then he sat behind his desk silently for a long time.

September 11, 9:30 A.M . IDT   Jerusalem

Abdul Jihad sauntered arrogantly down the street, feeling the huge bulk of the Desert Eagle pistol stuck in the waistband of his trousers comfortingly cool against his stomach under his loose linen shirt. The damn Jews did make a wonderful gun, you had to give them that. And carrying it ensured that he would be shown the proper respect by his comrades. Respect was important. More than important — vital, if you were going to survive in the Byzantine world of shifting allegiances that was the Palestinian resistance against the Jew occupiers of holy Jerusalem and the other Arab lands. After all, respect was why he had changed his name. Abdul of the Holy War was a great improvement over Abdul al-Bakkar, Abdul the Cow. Especially if you were only fourteen years old.

He knew all about the Jews. They let his family rot in the Khan Yunis refugee camp in the Gaza strip. They bombed the buildings and bulldozed people's homes. He knew that only Hamas, the true believers, provided schools and medical care, not the Jew occupiers. The

Hamas school had taught him how to read, how to do arithmetic, and had also taught him about politics. He had learned how the Jews had stolen the land in 1948, how they had only done it because the cursed rich Americans had bribed the United Nations to partition Palestine. He had learned at the mosque that the Jews were not even human, that they were the spawn of pigs and monkeys. He had learned that they all deserved to die.

Hamas had smuggled him out of Gaza and sent him to Jerusalem to join in *jihad*. It had selected him after an outburst in his class. "We shoot rockets at them that don't hit anything, and then they attack us with fighter planes. Palestinians die, and the Jews sleep peacefully in their beds! They treat us like animals. We get no respect! It makes me ashamed! We should destroy them!" At worst, he expected to die as a *shahid*, a martyr, and enjoy eternal life in Paradise. Seventy virgins sounded pretty good to a boy just going through puberty. And twenty-five-thousand American dollars if he was sent to Paradise was more than sufficient to assure his family's blessing.

And how much more respect he would have after today! To hell with the orders to stop the attacks during some stupid talks. We won't get our state by talking, he thought — we'll get it by driving the damn Jews back into the sea. And I will bring the war to where they really live this time. Not just to some pathetic little West Bank settlement.

He noted with satisfaction that women grabbed their children and shrank back into the shadows when he passed. It was only proper that they do so when confronting a warrior of Allah like himself. He kept a weather eye out for any unattended young women walk-ing alone. Not for any selfish, personal sexual purpose, but to remember them for future punishment. The new Islamic Palestinian State would not tolerate immorality.

He reached into his pockets and felt the solid bulk of the extra magazines. He smiled to himself. He was ready. It was almost time.

September 11, 10:00 A.M . IDT Jerusalem

Hannah's building, all concrete and cantilevered bal-conies, didn't have much character. The entrance to the lobby of the high rise on Strauss Street was reached by climbing four square stairs from the sidewalk and open-ing a plain tempered glass door. But her apartment, a one bedroom on the eighth floor, was a welcome contrast. Hannah had an artistic streak and a little money, and it showed. The living/dining room furniture was elegant, Kastiel designs that combined classic lines with mod-ern materials. The walls were decorated with Chagall prints. The bedroom was almost completely filled by a king-sized Hastens bed, an insane extravagance that she appreciated more each night. Especially when she was not alone.

Colonel Zvi ben-Aryeh lay comfortably on his back, the white cotton sheet pulled up just above his navel, his right hand putting a Marlboro cigarette to his lips. He wasn't too crazy about America, but their cigarettes were a lot better than the domestic ones, like the Noblesse cough machines. His left hand rested companionably on Hannah's flank as she lay naked beside him, her back-side pressed firmly against his hip. He gave her flesh a gentle, friendly pinch, then a little pat. It was always so good with Hannah, he thought dreamily. It was almost like being married again. He forced the thought away. It brought up too many painful memories.

He put out the cigarette, then rolled over on his side and wrapped his right arm around Hannah's quiet form. He kissed her neck, and she stirred easily, pushing herself closer against him. He kissed her again and she rolled over toward him, wrapping her arms around his neck and giving him an amused look. "Again?" He grinned back at her. "And why not?" thinking even as he did so how typical it was for a Jew to answer a question with a question. Even that question.

A little later, as they were dressing, he flicked on the flat screen Sony television hanging on the wall above the dresser. She raised her eyebrows at him. "Zvi, you are such a news junkie! Do you have to look at that thing now?" He waved her away gently. In his line of business, it was a good idea to know what was going on all the time. The screen showed some uninteresting pictures of old men milling about in a corridor. The newscaster was saying "In a stormy Cabinet meeting last night, Prime Minister Jacob Sorkin announced his decision to proceed with talks with the members of the Arab League to begin drafting a comprehensive peace settlement. The controversial proposal, involving the creation of a Palestinian State in Judaea and Samaria and in the Gaza Strip, is supported by a paper-thin majority in the Knesset. Only time will tell whether a concrete agreement embodying the principles of the Arab League proposal and still guaranteeing our security can actually be worked out." Colonel ben-Aryeh shut off the TV disgustedly. Politicians! They would agree to anything, then leave it up to the Army to guarantee security. His job was going to be lots of fun with a Palestinian Army poised to strike seven miles from the sea! Oh well, he thought, we handled it before 1967, we can handle it again.

Hannah slipped up behind him and draped her arms down his chest, crossing them and squeezing not quite hard enough to hurt. She bit his ear. "Come on," she said, "let's go out for a walk! It's a beautiful day, and I'm full of energy." He hugged her again. They dressed, then walked out the apartment door, took the elevator down to the lobby, and walked out onto Strauss Street.

The streets were full of people. Colonel ben-Aryeh and Hannah ambled pleasantly back in the direction of the King David. They paid no attention to the skinny Arab kid walking toward them, looking casually at the shop fronts.

And then, just as they passed in front of the hotel doors, it happened. To Colonel ben-Aryeh, it seemed to occur in a horrible kind of slow motion. He saw the kid reach under his shirt, then there was a gun in his hand and he was shooting randomly into the crowd, the huge bullets from the Desert Eagle pistol mushrooming as they hit and throwing great gouts of blood onto the walls and sidewalks. Colonel ben-Aryeh could feel himself throwing Hannah to the ground, trying to cover her with his body to protect her when there was the sickening thud of a bullet striking flesh, and he saw her head snap to one side as her neck exploded redly. And all through the chaos he could hear the Arab youth screaming "*Allah akbar! Allah akbar!* God is great! God is great!" And then, finally, he could hear the chattering of an Uzi, see the Arab jerking as the bullets hit him, see him collapse to the ground. He turned back to where Hannah's broken body lay on the sidewalk, an ocean of blood still flowing from her neck, her eyes glazed in death. Colonel ben-Aryeh wanted to weep his eyes out, but somehow he could do nothing but stare. Almost in a trance, he got to his feet and ran across the street to where the Arab lay on the sidewalk, surrounded by police and soldiers. He whipped out his identification and forced his way over to the Arab sprawled on the ground. Amazingly, the boy wasn't dead, wasn't even unconscious. Colonel ben-Aryeh knelt and looked down at him in disbelief. So young, this one, so young to kill my Hannah. Does he have any idea what he's done? He leaned over the boy and said one word: "Why?" He didn't expect an answer, and almost missed it when it came. "Because Allah demands it, that is why," whispered the boy. The boy closed his eyes. An ambulance pulled up and the medics lifted him onto a stretcher and rolled it inside. Lights flashing, siren howling, the ambulance sped off into the night.

Colonel ben-Aryeh stood up. He felt dizzy, and there was a cold lump in his chest. How can you fight fanaticism, he wondered, when you can't kill an idea, even a sick, poisonous idea? He wandered dazedly down the street, waving away offers of help, and then suddenly he was lying on the ground and people were hovering over him. He tried to sit up, but it was too hard. The scene spun faster and faster around his head, and then there was blessed blackness.

September 11, 9:00 P.M. IDT   Jerusalem

Hussein Musawi sipped slowly at the sweet mint tea. It was the only indulgence he permitted himself, and so it was to be savored. The others waited respectfully for him to finish. It was cool and dark in the little cellar room. The hard-packed dirt floor exuded a pleasantly musty odor which mixed with the smell of petroleum lubricant and harsh metal to produce the ineffable aroma of conspiracy. Despite the spying by the Shin Bet, despite the patrols and security checks, Hamas had successfully established an operations base in Israel. Ten feet above them, the Arab quarter of the Old City of Jerusalem churned obliviously on.

Musawi finished his tea and put the empty glass on the corner of the rough wooden table. He leaned back in the swivel chair, and fingered the cast metal handle of the Fairbairn Sykes commando dagger he kept sheathed on his belt. Not that he planned to use the dagger this evening. But it kept their attention to see him fondle it gently, like a woman's breasts. They had seen him use it before when discipline needed to be enforced.

His grey eyes, magnified to robin's egg size by the thick bifocal lenses of his wire-rimmed spectacles, flickered rapidly around the table, appraising the half dozen fighters sitting easily around it. Young but good, these men, not one over 20 years old but all veterans of dozens of skirmishes with the hated Israeli occupiers. All of them physically stronger than a balding, slightly paunchy, middle-aged doctor, he thought ruefully. He caught the momentary weakness, and hastily appended another thought: but not tougher. And right now, tough was infinitely more important than strong.

He started to talk, his voice almost a whisper, but a penetrating whisper with the sibilance of a snake. The men were deathly silent, straining to catch every word, every syllable of each divinely inspired phrase. "Soldiers of Islam, our brothers are within days of selling us out. They prepare to sign a peace treaty that consigns us to a powerless, fragmented, disarmed shadow of a state. When they have drunk deep at the poisonous well of Western corruption they seek from the Israeli usurpers, they will abandon the true teaching, and they will abandon us. We cannot allow this to come to pass."

The men around the table reflexively nodded agreement. They knew that the coming peace would spell the end of their dream of a resurgent Islamic Palestine leading the Arab world to a glorious, bloody victory. Musawi rocked forward gently in his chair and extended his arms on the table. They were slender arms, delicately muscled, with just a light down of greying hair covering the backs. A massive stainless steel chronograph on an expansion band encircled his left wrist. It was a soldier's watch, not a doctor's, but he permitted himself this little chink in the armor of innocuousness with which he wrapped himself in his public persona. No one at the hospital really even noticed it, never sensed the incongruity. But it was a tangible symbol for him of his devotion to *jihad*, something he could touch and feel during the dull days of smiling subservience to a repugnant political order that separated the necessarily rare bouts of action. Let his hands appear to his fellow staff members to be devoted to healing the cursed Jews. He could glance down at his watch and know better.

His mind drifted back to his fifteenth year. Life as an Arab in Israel had not been bad. He went to school, studied hard, and thought about becoming a doctor. It wasn't a crazy dream. His family lived comfortably, and would support his education. But he was very smart, and smart kids attract attention.

At the close of one algebra class, his teacher, Achmed Sahuri, had asked him to stay for a few minutes. Why not? It was the last class of the day, and he was not in any particular hurry to get home. The teacher, dressed in an open necked linen shirt and white canvas pants, pulled a chair over next to the desk that sat squarely at the front of the room below the blackboard. The desk surface was cluttered with papers waiting to be graded. Sahuri told him to sit down. "Hussein, I want to talk to you about your future," he said, looking past Musawi through the window to the schoolyard below, where a group of boys were playing soccer. "You're very bright. You know that. You have the talent to do anything you want. But do you know how what you do will help your people?" Musawi thought that was a straightforward question. "I want to be a doctor, Mr. Sahuri, to help sick people." The teacher shook his head. "That's not what I asked you. I asked how are you going to help people, the Arabs?" Musawi hadn't thought about his future that way. "I'm going to help everybody. That's what a doctor does." The teacher paused for a moment. "You have a greater obligation than that. There is a special study group that I and some friends have organized. It meets twice a week after school at the Abdeen Mosque. I want you to join the group." Musawi was not particularly religious, and said so. "I don't think that's for me. What would we study?" The teacher smiled. "Come to one class. If you are not interested, you can stop any time. We will study the important things: Islam, history, politics. It will open up a whole new world to you."

It did.

At the close of classes the next day, Musawi joined Mr. Sahuri and walked to the mosque. The *muezzin's* call to the afternoon *'Asr* prayer, the third prayer of the five required each day, echoed down from a loudspeaker in the minaret. The two of them removed their shoes, entered the mosque, and dropped to their knees on one of the ornate prayer rugs scattered about the floor. Although Musawi was not very religious, he had learned the daily prayers, and the ritual sequence of obeisances, rocking forward to touch his head to the ground at the traditional intervals. When the prayers had been completed, Musawi and his teacher both rose to their feet, walked across the main room and down a narrow corridor, and entered a small classroom already filled with other boys Musawi's age, sitting on the parquet floor with their legs crossed. Mr. Sahuri said "Go sit with the others, Hussein," and walked to the front of the room to join another man who was standing next to a table piled with pamphlets. The other man was dressed like the clean shaven Mr. Sahuri, but in contrast had a ragged full black beard streaked with grey. He spoke. "I see we have a new man with us today. *Ahlan wa sahlan*, Welcome!" Musawi was surprised and flattered. It was the first time anyone had ever called him a man, not a boy. "You have joined us on a particularly good day, because today we are going to begin our study of the real history of Palestine during the Occupation." He turned to the table, picked up a pile of pamphlets, and handed it to one of the boys to distribute. Hussein took his copy of the pamphlet. On the cover was a line drawing of an

Israeli soldier with the face of a pig and a Swastika on the sleeve of his uniform, sticking a bayonet dripping with blood into the belly of a pregnant woman. Hussein was revolted, but simultaneously fascinated. Did this kind of thing actually happen? He turned the pamphlet over. The back cover was blank except for one line at the bottom which said in Arabic "Printed in Saudi Arabia." He turned back to the front of the pamphlet as the bearded man said "Let us now turn to the first page." Hussein began to learn.

Musawi's reverie ended. His head jutted forward like that of a striking serpent, matching his voice. "How is this disaster to be stopped, this surrender to the corrupt concept that the Zionists can remain on our land? Not by simple isolated acts of terror. Our little brother Abdul Jihad was rash, unproductively rash. The time is past for such tiny gestures.

"The traitorous scum who claim to represent the Palestinian people and the people of the Arab states seek to make peace for one reason and one reason only. They despair of achieving military victory. Why have they lost hope? Because of the Israeli nuclear arsenal. Even when we, too, have the bomb, fear of Israeli retaliation will unman them.

"But what would happen, my soldiers, if the front-line states knew that the Israeli nuclear threat had been turned against them and had destroyed the financial and commercial heart of the Zionist entity? Would not our brothers seize their opportunity to strike, courageously, remorselessly, victoriously? Is not this the true way?" Hussein Musawi did not need to hear an answer he already knew. His eyes gleamed with the certainty of the True Believer in the One True Faith. His men stared at him, rapt and trembling. Never before had they heard their leader speak with such intensity. Musawi's voice dropped even lower, so that his listeners had to strain to catch the words. "Soldiers of Islam, now is not the time for noisy bravado. Now is the time for cunning."

CHAPTER 3

September 24 11:30 A.M. *. IDT   Jerusalem*

Colonel ben-Aryeh woke up surrounded by white: white ceiling, white sheets, a white curtain hanging from a stainless steel rail and pulled back to reveal a woman dressed in white sitting in a chair reading a magazine. As he became more fully conscious, he realized that he was in a hospital bed. There were flowers on a table by the bedside. The nurse jumped up as he stirred, walked over and scanned the digital screen linked by a tangle of wires to his arm and his scalp, then hurried out into the corridor. She returned a minute later with a bearded young doctor, stethoscope and all. The doctor looked earnestly at him as he asked "What do you remember, Colonel?" It all came flooding back: the shooting, Hannah falling, the fanatic babbling of the gunman. "Everything, I think. There was shooting, then Hannah was dead, then I talked to the Arab, then I must have fainted. Right?" The doctor nodded noncommittally. "That's right, Colonel, as far as it goes. It's just that after you fainted, you stayed unconscious for two weeks. How do you feel?" Colonel ben-Aryeh felt alright and said so. The doctor made some chicken scratchings on his chart. Then he and the nurse left.

Colonel ben-Aryeh stared uncomprehendingly at the ceiling. Unconscious for two weeks. Unbelievable. Two weeks of his life vanished forever. What had happened while he was gone who knew where? He reached across to the chair where the nurse had been sitting and picked up her news magazine. There on the cover was the smiling face of Jacob Sorkin, grasping the hand of the grinning Palestinian leader, with a headline shrieking "Almost There!" Almost there, he thought, the sword of Islam ready to be plunged into the heart of Israel. His head began to ache, and the room shimmered a little, but he fought the feeling back. He thought about the Arab boy's voice, the eternal death promised by his eyes. How do you kill an idea? he wondered again. But this time, he began to see the beginning of an answer.

The nurse returned with an orderly dressed in blue scrubs who wheeled him out of the room, down the featureless hospital corridor, and into the first of many diagnostic chambers. At the end of the process, his bed was rolled into an equally anonymous examining room, flat tan paint on the walls, and recessed fluorescent lights in the ceiling. Around the perimeter of the room were stainless steel tables stacked with tongue depressors, cotton swabs, and other assorted instruments of torture. Colonel ben-Aryeh rolled onto the examining table and let the doctor poke him. The doctor finished poking and grunted. "Still feeling all right, Colonel?" "No complaints, doctor, none at all, except for boredom. I want to get back to duty. Any reason why I shouldn't?"

The doctor grunted again, noncommittally. That's the question, he thought to himself, is there any reason to disqualify this officer from anything. He was damned if he could find anything physically wrong. The Colonel

seemed fit enough now. It wasn't all that unusual to collapse from shock, especially considering the series of
tragedies this man had been through. It would be almost
criminal to deny him his work, the one thing left to him.
And yet... it was damned unusual to go out for that long.
And there was something about the Colonel that was
strange, really strange, but you couldn't put your finger
on it. The doctor shrugged. Well, I'm not a witch doctor, he thought, I'm not going to make this call on vague
instincts. I'm going to let this soldier get back to his war.

Colonel ben-Aryeh was still waiting for the doctor's answer. "No, Colonel, no reason that I can think
of. I'm returning you to full duty status. I'll notify your
commanding officer." They shook hands and another
orderly helped the Colonel into a wheelchair and rolled
him through the examination room door and back to
his hospital room. Someone had sent for his clothing. He
dressed quickly and then sat in the chair next to the bed
and read the newspaper until the nurse came by with his
hospital discharge papers. He thanked her, then left the
hospital and took a taxicab back to his apartment.

He walked up the bare stairwell, down the carpeted
corridor, and through the door of his three-room apartment. Its emptiness screamed at him. Empty forever,
he thought, empty because of them. Empty because of
their blind, fanatical hatred. Empty because of their
faith, their diabolical, fiendish, hateful faith. Enough!
He might spend the rest of his life in meaningless emptiness, alone, unloved, unloving, but he would have his
revenge. He would take something even greater away
from them, all of them, now and forever. He would
destroy their faith by destroying its tangible symbol.
They are different from us, he thought. We lasted two

thousand years without a tie to our land. But they are like salmon, returning every year to spawn. Year after year, thousand upon thousand, million upon million, they return to Mecca. They live in hope of making the *Haj*, the sacred pilgrimage. Once they have made it, they are of the elect. Until they have made it, they live in hope. Well, not any more, you animals, not ever again. Never again.

He sat at the white metal kitchen table with the red trim, a lined yellow pad in front of him. Methodically, he began to list the security procedures that prevented the launch of a nuclear-armed Israeli missile. Next to each procedure he listed the names of the men who could override it. He read the names over carefully, reviewing everything he knew of each man. It was quite a lot. Finally, next to a few names, he carefully drew a six-pointed star.

October 5 6:00 P.M. EST   New York

It was cold for a New York October. The wind whipping off the Hudson River carried a wet chill that surged through the Columbia University campus. David Hirsh was on his way back from his four o'clock philosophy class, shoulders hunched, chin tucked tightly in over the taut drawstring of his hooded grey and blue Columbia sweatshirt. He was trotting down the steps in front of Kent Hall on his way back to Furnald Dorm when he noticed her sitting all alone in front of the statue of Alma Mater, knees drawn up under folded arms, head resting on the backs of her forearms, radiating despair. It was almost dark, a bad time for a girl to be out alone, even inside the campus, with the seething tide of Spanish Harlem only a few blocks away.

David walked over to her and stood looking down, his Eastern Mountain Sports knapsack hung casually over his left shoulder. She didn't look up, so he cleared his throat softly. Her head snapped up as if she had been hit under the chin with a roundhouse uppercut. She was very pretty. Light olive skin, deep black eyes, lips full and red without benefit of makeup. David jumped back a little, saying "Whoa, hey, sorry, I didn't mean to frighten you. Is everything all right?"

She looked as if she had been crying, not tragically, just miserably. She tried to compose herself. "Yes, sure, everything's fine." Her voice had a slight foreign accent. David gave her a friendly grimace. "Right, you always cry because everything's all right." She managed a weak smile. "Well, maybe everything is not fine. But I don't want to bother you with it." David was mildly encouraged. At least she hadn't told him it was none of his business. And she was certainly pretty.

"Come on," he said, "you can worry inside as well as outside. This is no time for anybody to be out alone." She sighed and stood up. "I suppose you're right." She started to walk away. David scampered to catch up with her, turning sideways, then backwards so he could see her expression. "Hey, look, have you had dinner yet? Because if you haven't, I haven't either, and maybe we could have dinner together, and you can talk about it, or not, I don't care, what do you say?" He found he was slightly out of breath. She stopped and smiled, a real smile this time, and then laughed. I overdid it, David thought. I must look like a puppy. But, unbelievably, she said "I would love to have dinner with you. And maybe

I will talk about it. It's not that terrible, I suppose. I'm flunking a course, and I'm afraid I'll lose my scholarship, and then I'll have to go home, and I want to stay here." "What's the course?" David asked. "Statistics for idiots. But I have to take it for my major. Psychology." She shook her head in disgust and continued, "Why they ask me to understand all those stupid symbols when all I want to do is work with children, escapes me. But I don't have a choice." David smiled sympathetically. "I know what you mean. But it really isn't so bad. You can learn it." He took a deep breath. "In fact, I can teach it to you if you like. I'm a business management major. I've had tons of statistics courses. Let's talk about it some more over dinner. It's cold just standing here. Oh, by the way, my name is David Hirsch." "Jasmine Mahdin" she replied as she took his arm, and they walked across campus to the student commons in John Jay Hall. The room was not very crowded, and they found a small table toward the end of the room away from the steam table and cafeteria line. They slid their trays onto the table, and David moved over behind her to help her with her chair. "It's a habit," he explained as he did so, "it doesn't mean I'm unliberated." She smiled up at him. "That's OK, I like it. In my country, women aren't always treated so nicely." A momentary frown passed over her face. "Oh? And where is that?" David asked, sitting down and beginning to unload his tray. "Lebanon," she said. Uh-oh, thought David Hirsh.

November 17, 4:00 P.M. EST   New York

The huge crowd on the lawn running between the Butler Library and the Low Library was seething with hatred, a roiling mass of hysteria and incipient violence. "Student" organizers with electronic bullhorns roamed through the mob, leading chants. Signs and banners were everywhere, their lettering carefully crafted to look amateurish, a spontaneous outpouring of grassroots indignation, with no hint that they had been prepared by employees of the Council on American Islamic Relations. Moderate signs: "Restore the Legitimate Rights of the Palestinian People." "Remove the Settlements." "Divest from Israel." And the not so moderate ones: "Liberate Jerusalem." "Annihilate Israel." "America, Your Time is Over." And of course, "Kill the Jews." Television cameras rolled, the cameramen roaming randomly through the mob, hoping for trouble. The Rally for Palestine was in full swing.

A stage had been erected at the Butler Library end of the lawn, courtesy of the Columbia administration, anxious to appear accommodating to avoid a repetition of the 1968 student riots. "An inclusive, diverse campus, where all voices can be heard" was their mantra. As Neville Chamberlin said, "We can do business with Hitler."

David Hirsch and Jasmine Mahdin watched the chaos through the window of the main reading room in Butler. And heard it too, since it was an unseasonably warm November and the window was partially open.

A speaker walked to the microphone. He was a tall man in his late twenties, pale complexion, curly black hair, wearing jeans and a T-shirt with the word "Justice" emblazoned on the front. He smiled at the crowd and began "I bring you greetings from the young Jewish community!" David did a double take. What the hell? He glanced at Jasmine, who looked as puzzled as he was. The speaker continued, "The Palestinian people have many friends in the Jewish community. And we of J-Street are at the forefront of the fight for your rights! You must not be misled by the racist words of AIPAC and the other so-called mainstream Jewish organizations. They are organizations of tired old men who refuse to recognize the new realities. Israel is the last European colonial power in the Middle East, and the time for colonialism is past. Your fight is a just fight. We wish you well!" He turned and sat down to wild applause.

David shook his head disgustedly. "J-Street! A cabal of self-hating Jewish progressives." He turned to Jasmine. "Can't they read the signs? Do they want to walk into the gas chambers again?" Jasmine put her arm around his shoulders. "Of course they don't want to commit suicide, David. They just believe that the best way to stay alive is to make peace on the best terms possible, but peace at any cost." She shrugged. "Who knows? Perhaps they are right."

David didn't think so.

March 3, 7:00 P.M. EST   New York

Sam Hirsh wasn't happy. He sat at the head of the dinner table, watching his fifteen year old son Aaron and eleven year old daughter Sarah prove that they had no table manners, and listened to his wife Barbara *kvetch*. Barbara loved to complain: about the furniture, about the drapes, about the plumber, about the Lexus, about *him*, especially. Usually, he didn't mind. Everybody needs a hobby, after all, and Barbara's complaints were so incessant and casual that he could ignore them and not have to pay later. But this time was different. This was a legitimate *kvetch*. In fact, if she hadn't been doing enough *kvetching* for both of them, he would have started *kvetching* himself.

"Sam! It's not right for David to be that friendly with a *shikse*, a non-Jewish girl! And worse, an Arab, for God's sake! Every time I call, it's Jasmine this, Jasmine that, Jasmine and I are going out to study, Jasmine and I are going to a movie, Jasmine and I are going out to share herpes!" That was a little much, even for Sam. He finally opened his mouth for a reason other than to stuff another knish in it. "Oh, come on, Barbara, David's a good boy. You don't have to get crude to make your point." Barbara slowed down, but only momentarily. Her hefty figure was shaking with righteous indignation, big breasts wobbling inside the yellow blouse with the appliqued curlicue design that Sam bet had cost three-hundred bucks at Bloomie's. Her chubby face shone with perspiration, and she waved a chicken drumstick at him for emphasis. "That's right, Sam, he is a good boy, *now*. I want him to stay that way. And that means I don't want him around that girl anymore!"

Sam sighed. She was right. He wanted an Arab daughter-in-law like he wanted another hemorrhoid. On the other hand, David was a pretty shrewd judge of people. If he liked this girl, there was something to her. Probably a lot. Sam slouched in his chair, tie askew, cuffs rolled up, and looked uncomfortably down at his paunch, squeezed between his hips and the table like a rubber watermelon. He pinched it with both hands, scowled, and then reached for another knish. Sam wasn't too good at cause and effect reasoning. Except in business.

"So what am I supposed to do, Barbara? Forbid him to see her? Don't be silly. In this day and age, you can't tell them anything. We're lucky it's a girl he's seeing." They thought about Jerry Brinstein's son and his boyfriend and shuddered at each other. But Barbara wasn't giving up so fast. "No, I don't want you to tell him not to see her. I'm not an idiot. But I do have an idea." Barbara's green eyes narrowed and her mouth pursed in the way Sam knew meant he was about to spend a lot of money. "He spent most of the Christmas break with her. I don't want him knocking around with nothing to do but see her for the entire summer vacation. So why don't we send him to visit his Cousin Sid in Israel? Sid's always asking to have him, and David would love it. And *she* isn't going to take a vacation there, that's for sure."

Sam had to admit it wasn't such a crazy idea. Besides, if the kid did a "site visit" at Abramowitz's diamond factory, a big chunk of the trip could be written off for tax purposes. Sam glanced hungrily over at Barbara's ample bosom. Also, he thought, if I go along quietly, it won't be such a bad night tonight...

April 10, 7:00 P.M. IDT   Jerusalem

Not every immigrant to Israel is happy that he came. Sergeant Shmuel Gradsteyn stood up from the kitchen table and pushed the chair back so hard that it toppled over, hitting the floor with a crash that made the baby break out into renewed screaming. Shit, this lousy apartment was worse than the one in Odessa. Ten years of waiting, ten years of starving and begging, for this? His khaki tank top undershirt was patchy with sweat, and sweat ran through the matted greying hair of his armpits like bedbugs. His wife Anna cowered in the corner, vainly trying to comfort the baby whose mind-wrenching shrieks rose to a crescendo of infantile insanity. "Goddamn you, you ugly bitch, shut that fucking kid up! You had to have a fucking kid, didn't you, it didn't make any difference that you're too goddamn old to keep it quiet, and I'm too goddamn old to listen to it!" He grabbed his dress shirt and started to pull it on as he ran out the door of the one-room apartment. He finished buttoning it as he ran down the dingy corridor, filled with the same smell of boiling cabbage that filled the halls of the crumbling apartment blocks of Russia, along with the same dirty children, the same goddamn squalid poverty. Why did he have to be a fucking Yid? Why couldn't he be a normal person?

Sergeant Gradsteyn barged out onto the street and ran three blocks to the café where he liked to get drunk, the one where all the Russian émigrés came so they could talk about old times. Maybe a Jew, but a Russian first, he thought, and a Russian needs vodka!

By the fourth drink, Sergeant Gradsteyn was happier, in a glum sort of way. He was at the point where he liked to talk about how important he was, about what a shit his commanding officer, Colonel ben-Aryeh, was, about how he could blow up the whole fucking world if he wanted to. Most people in the café ignored him. But one of them had been listening to his babblings for months. Tonight, he planned to do more than listen. He walked over to the drunken sergeant and sat down next to him, sliding a full glass over in front of him as he did so. "*Za vasha starovya!*" bellowed Sergeant Gradsteyn, and drained his glass. "*Za vasha*" responded Hussein Musawi, sipping his sweet mint tea.

April 11, 7:00 P.M. AST   Riyadh

The per capita income of Saudi Arabia is $25,000 per year, about one-half that in the United States. So why does everyone think that Saudi Arabia is a fabulously rich country? Because most of the capita don't get any income, so that the few that *do* get an incredibly vast amount, and aren't shy about showing it. As Mel Brooks says, "It's good to be the King."

Prince Salman bin Talal, Minister of Defense of the Kingdom of Saudi Arabia, walked purposefully down the ornately decorated corridor in the Royal Palace. The floor was covered with an enormous blue and gold carpet, the loops and curlicues inspired by fruits and flowers. The ceiling twenty feet above was covered with a mosaic of blue and green tiles. The white walls were interrupted at frequent intervals by gilded pilasters on which were hung enormous urns. Prince bin Talal was very young to be a top Saudi Arabian official, only 63. His predecessor had been 78 at the time of his replacement by bin Talal. Bin Talal had an abrasive confrontational style, very much at variance with usual Arab courtesy. He was dressed in traditional attire, long white robe and a white headdress held in shape by a circular braided black rope running around his head just above his ears. Traditional dress was appropriate, because he was about to meet with the King.

Bin Talal entered King Yamani's working office. The contrast with the corridor was striking. The King sat behind a modern highly polished wooden desk, papers stacked in trays spread across the large surface. He was bent over a yellow legal pad, writing with an unremarkable Bic ballpoint pen. The King looked up as Bin Talal entered the room. "*Assalam alaikum*, Peace be unto you, Prince Salman. I am anxious to hear what has caused you to make a request to chat privately." "*Alaikum assalam*, your Majesty" replied bin Talal, standing back a respectful distance. "I thank you for granting me this time. An unprecedented opportunity has presented itself that will allow us to reassert control over the whole of the Arab world, and to counter the threat posed by the Shiite heretics in Iran. I will be requesting your permission to pursue this opportunity." The King leaned back into the padding of his chair, and tented his fingers. It was his customary posture of intense concentration. "And what is this opportunity?"

Bin Talal took a deep breath and began. "Your Majesty, We have not yet developed a nuclear weapon. Our hesitation has been caused by the intolerable pressure placed upon us by the American infidels. While they have no real power over us, commercial reasons and reasons of state have made us acquiesce. And it has been impossible for us to proceed covertly, because the physical dimensions of a nuclear weapon facility are very great; the specialized equipment necessary can only be obtained from other countries; and the time required is several years. Complete secrecy in today's world of electronic surveillance and financial transaction monitoring cannot be achieved. If we did attempt to proceed, the Americans would know, and they would throw roadblocks in our path that would stretch the time to complete the project even further into the future.

"However, there is now another path available to us, a quick and easy path, a path that will leave the Americans in the dark until it is far too late for them to do anything about it. The Americans' obsession with Afghanistan has caused them to step too far over the line. Their drone attacks on the tribal areas have infuriated the Pakistani government, and in particular the ISI. The worldwide economic depression has decimated the Pakistani export industry, and the government is starving for cash. I have been approached by General Shapoor Zadran, the head of the ISI. He has been authorized to offer us twenty nuclear weapons for a price of twenty billion dollars. It is a pittance! We currently have over five hundred billion dollars in gold and foreign exchange reserves.

"General Zadran knows that we are prudent business men. He proposes that he first send us a single weapon to be examined by our experts as a show of good faith. When they are satisfied, we will transfer one billion dollars to the Pakistani treasury. We will then repeat this procedure until all the weapons have been sold to us.

"Your Majesty, the time to act is now! Iran will have a nuclear bomb within the year. If they announce that they have become a nuclear power before we become one, they will exploit their military advantage instantly to peel away our allies and leave us isolated. If the world-wide economy recovers, the financial desperation driving the Pakistanis will abate, and the opportunity will evaporate. I urge you to instruct me to go forward."

The King sat silently for a full ten minutes. He then exercised the prerogative available only to an autocrat. "Do it," he said, and turned back to his papers.

CHAPTER 4

June 15, 4:00 P.M. EDT　　　　***New York***

I t was an old smell in the Delancey Street *shtiebel*, the little synagogue that somehow, against all reason, survived in a Lower East Side in which the Jewish community had been all but completely displaced by the succeeding waves of immigration. It was a smell compounded of old *talesim*, prayer shawls of wool, not silk, that had been used for twenty thousand days; of prayer books that had been handled by a hundred thousand hands, a million worn fingers; of wilted black rayon *yarmulkes*, skullcaps that had rested on tens of thousands of heads, curly black, grizzled grey, bald, sweaty; of musty cushions on rock hard wooden benches. To a stranger, especially a *goy*, a non-Jewish person, it would be strange, perhaps depressing, even revolting. To David Hirsh, it was comfortable, it was reassuring, it was real, it was home. David stood next to his grandfather, *davening*, bobbing front to back, twisting from side to side, in the rhythmic genuflection that traditionally accompanies Jewish prayer. His lips moved slightly as he subvocalized the old words, only a slight hum broken by an occasional intake of breath escaping his lips as he flipped rapidly through the book's pages. He finished, closed the book, kissed it, and put it back in the rack attached to the seat in front of him. Then he sat down and waited for his grandfather to finish. A minute later, his grandfather completed his prayers and repeated the same ritual of closing and kissing the book. He sat down next to David and gave him a stylized dirty look: eyes narrowed, lips pursed, head turned to the side. "So, big shot, you finished first! Wait until you got bifocals, like me. We'll see how fast you finish." Then he couldn't hold the pose any longer. He broke into a grin, threw his arm around David's shoulder, and squeezed. "Not bad, *boy-chik*. You *daven* like a pro."

They rose and walked out the door into the pleas-ant warmth of a June evening. David's grandfather's old Pontiac was drawn up to the curb. They got in and headed out across the 59th Street bridge, out to David's home in Oceanside. David's grandfather turned up the air conditioner. It made a lot of noise, but didn't cool much. David squirmed in the heat. His grandfather glanced over at him and shook his head in mock dis-pleasure. "*Oi*, such a sissy!" He sighed. "Get used to the heat. You're going to spend next *Shabbes*, the Sabbath, in the Holy Land."

"I know, Zayde. I'm really looking forward to it. It was a wonderful thing for my parents to do, to send me, even if they did have an ulterior motive." He glanced sideways at his grandfather, who made a wry face. "Yeah, yeah, getting you away from your *shikse* girlfriend. Look, David, I'll tell you something. I want you to make a Jewish home as much as your parents do. Maybe more, even. But maybe you can do that with this girl, too. The Torah is full of Jewish men who married *shikses*: Moses, King David, King Solomon. The point is, David, she's got to join *us*; you can't join *them*. Keep that in mind, and maybe everything will work out." He was quiet for a long time, and they both stared out the windshield, watching the taillights of the traffic make long red lines weaving hypnotically into the distance. Then, abruptly, he started to talk again. "I think you'll have a wonderful time in Israel, David. But I want you to be very sure not to get fuzzy headed. You're not going to any Land of Milk and Honey. It's not a musical comedy over there. There's a war on. You watch your *tuchis*, your backside, while you're there. You remember how to protect yourself, and don't take any wooden nickels!" The quaint, old-fashioned phrase should have been ludicrous; it wasn't. In the darkness, as the car rolled out toward Long Island, carrying David toward tomato juice and rib roast and potatoes and cookies and tea and tomorrow morning to the land of his ancestors ten thousand miles away, it was somehow chilling.

June 16, 7:00 P.M. EDT Washington, D.C.

President Norris Lippincott sat in the club chair with the traditional vaguely floral pattern across from the modern beige sofa with the contrasting geometric black zigzags on a beige base in the private residence of the White House. The white Palladian window behind the sofa was framed by floor-to-ceiling drapes color-coordinated with the sofa. "A hundred thousand dollars certainly buys some sweet furniture," he thought. A hundred thousand dollars is the decorating allowance given to each incoming occupant of the Oval Office. Your tax dollars at work.

Next to his chair was a circular mahogany table with carved detailing around the edge, on which rested a black speakerphone. Jennifer Levine, Lippincott's chief of staff and main political advisor; Ted Howard, the Secretary of Defense; and Addison Cutler, the Secretary of State, sat on the couch. On a highly polished coffee table in front of the sofa were spread out, what else, coffee table books: "The Drawings of Michelangelo," "A Day in the Life of America," and others of that ilk. The kind of books one never reads.

The President liked to hold informal meetings in the private residence. They didn't go on the official calendar, and the press usually did not get wind of them. You just called a few friends and asked them over for a cup of coffee. It was the ideal location for making policy decisions that you didn't want bruited about until they were implemented and it was too late for the outcry by the loudmouths to have any effect.

The President leaned back in his chair, the base of his neck resting comfortably against the brocade. He had to force himself to appear relaxed whenever he had to discuss the Middle East. What an insane sewer it was, populated by the most obnoxious people on the face of the earth. He would much rather talk to the Russians. "I had a particularly unpleasant conversation with Sorkin this morning. He absolutely refuses to give us any kind of commitment that the Israelis will not carry out a pre-emptive attack on Iran over their nuclear program. He will not even undertake to give us a head's up if they decide to go forward. And he sounded like it was more when than if." The President lifted his head off the back of the chair and stared at the people sitting on the couch.

"We need to ratchet the pressure way up on those crazy bastards. I need ideas."

Secretary Howard was a big man in his early sixties, white-haired, with a red nose that looked like it came from excessive drinking, which it did not. Although he had removed his dark blue pinstriped suit jacket before sitting down, his white shirt and tightly knotted red tie gave the businesslike impression that he tried to maintain at all times. Before being recruited into Lippincott's administration, he had been the chief executive officer of the largest aircraft manufacturer in the country. He was now the chief executive officer of the most powerful military organization in the world. And he firmly believed that the methods that worked in business also worked in international relations. "Mr. President," he began, "there is only one thing that Jews understand and respect: money. If you want to have any effect, you need to hit them in their pocketbook. And we have a number of important pressure points. We can massively reduce charitable contributions to Israel by Americans, by having the IRS classify them as political contributions and removing their tax deductibility. We can impose huge "emergency" tariffs on all Israeli imports. You can issue an Executive Order canceling every contract the U.S. government has with an Israeli firm. Let them know we are about to crash their economy and they will cave in like a pricked balloon."

Lippincott glanced over at Jennifer Levine. Her black hair was pulled back in a severe bun, and she wore her customary sour face. She was a slender woman, almost seventy, and affected peasant dresses that made her actually look like, well, a peasant. Her fashion sense had been developed when she was a student radical at the University of Chicago in the sixties, and it had never changed. She was the consummate back-room, back-stabbing politician, who believed in Vince Lombardi's dictum: "Winning isn't the most important thing. It's the only thing." Anything that worked was acceptable: legal, illegal, honest, dishonest, fair, foul, it didn't matter. And Jennifer knew what worked.

"The ideas aren't bad. We're not going to get any back talk from the IRS. Commissioner Hornstein owes me for keeping his son out of the newspaper, and they can fast track a revenue ruling in a week. Even if we get sued for lack of due process, just issuing the ruling will turn off the fat-cat donors. That will get their attention. But the other two items are trickier. Too many of our major contributors are hooked up with Israeli companies one way or another, and we'll hurt them as much as we hurt the Israelis. I think tariffs and contract cutoffs will kill our fundraising, and we're going to need all the money we can get if we are going to get you re-elected."

Lippincott turned to the Secretary of State. Addison Cutler was State Department through and through, not that he looked it. He was balding, he was short, he was fat, he sweated. Bad physical genes. But his social genes were impeccable. Episcopal Church, Groton, Yale, Harvard Law, and twenty years rotating through the most important country desks, England, Russia, and finally Saudi Arabia. Israel didn't fit very well into the nice neat world he wanted to create.

"Norris, I think we're going at this from the wrong direction." He and the President had been classmates at Yale, so he was granted the special privilege of address-ing him by his first name. "Israel has been a dangerous irritant in the Middle East since 1947. They were useful as an ally during the Cold War. But they poison our relations with the Muslim states, and we need good relations with the Muslim states a great deal more than we need good relations with a noisy crowd of socialist Jews. We need Muslim oil. Even if we silence the tree-huggers, we cannot expand our domestic production fast enough to compensate for the permanent loss of Arab oil. We don't need anything from the Israelis.

"Israel cannot possibly win a war with Iran. From our point of view, the best thing that could happen would be an Israel-Iran war that removes Israel from the Middle East equation. Permanently. Our best course is to temporize, vaguely indicate our support for their existence, and then quietly let the Iranians and the other Muslim states know that we are going to go fishing while the Iranians finish them off. Let AIPAC and the other loud-mouthed Jews howl! Jews make up only one percent of the voters, and most of them don't care about Israel anyway. With Israel gone, we can stop worrying about the Middle East for a few decades."

The President turned again to Jennifer Levine. "Well, Jennifer? Your thoughts?"

Jennifer Levine was not crazy about being a Jew. She would have much preferred being a member of a respected majority than of a despised minority. But you don't get a choice. And as long as she *was* a Jew, she was not going to sit quietly while this pseudo-aristocratic little anti-Semitic prick advocated genocide against the Israelis. The Israelis were bastards, but they were *her* bastards.

Jennifer smiled. Addison Cutler felt his chest knot. Jennifer Levine only smiled when she expected to draw blood, a lot of blood. "It's a fantasy, Mr. President, and a dangerous fantasy at that. Addison spends too much time at his estate in Virginia. He does not have a clue what the actual impact of this policy would be. The Arabs will always hate us, with or without Israel in their midst, but they will always need our money. Getting rid of Israel will not get rid of mosquitos like *al Qaida*, but that is what they are, mosquitos, not grizzly bears. The Arabs and the Iranians cannot afford to permanently cut off our oil.

"But they *can* afford to cut off our oil for a few months, and that's just what will happen if the Israelis attack Iran. *We* can't afford it. Another oil shock like in seventy-three and seventy-nine would drive us into another deep recession. If that happens, you can kiss your chances of reelection goodbye. Addison's nonsense is a formula for political disaster for you personally. If you want to be reelected, you're going to need to send him back to his real job as your messenger boy, limit the policy discussions to the grownups, and make damn sure there is no Middle East War. I think we should initiate the charitable deduction ploy. But the other thing we should do is to let Sorkin know that if he tries to launch a pre-emptive strike, he's going to find American fighter jets stopping him."

June 18, 2:00 P.M. IDT   **Jerusalem**
The heat slapped David's face like the blast from a blow-torch as he shouldered his way through the glass doors of the international terminal at Jerusalem's Ben Gurion Airport. He staggered slightly under the weight of the enormous, scuffed tan leather suitcase with the double

handles he grasped grimly in his right hand. Ugh, he thought, that's the last time I let Mom help me pack! I could move to Bulgaria with all the junk she made me *shlepp* along.

David reached the curb and dropped the suitcase heavily to the concrete. He stretched his arm out and wiggled it, trying to flex some feeling back into the over-loaded wrist and shoulder. He squinted blearily into the glare, which made his head hurt even more than the remainder of the hangover he had bought himself by drinking a whole bottle of Israeli wine during dinner. He hadn't gotten much of a chance to sleep it off during the flight. Not that *that* was really his fault — who can sleep when there are three babies on the plane, scream-ing their lungs out in shifts?

David reached into the pocket of his plaid, short-sleeved shirt and pulled out the piece of paper with his Cousin Sid's address written on it in English and Hebrew. He was about to walk over to the information booth to find out where to catch the right bus when the guy swooped down on him like a New York pigeon on a fallen piece of soft pretzel.

"So, you need some help, yes? You just got in, yes? You need a ride to the city, yes? Where? Does it say on this piece of paper? You show it to me, yes?" David saw the paper with Sid Goldman's address being pulled out of his fingers by a grimy hand with heavy black hair on the backs of the pudgy knuckles. His eyes continued past the hand down the heavily tanned attached arm to the rest of the person making all the noise.

He was about forty years old, and the fifty extra pounds he was carrying on his five foot four inch frame marched ahead of him like a pregnant woman's tummy, rolling the top of his khaki pants over his belt. A hairy patch of skin showed through the opening below the bottom button of his dark green shirt. He held the piece of paper about two inches in front of his nose, and peered at it from under the brim of a black corduroy cap through horn-rimmed spectacles with lenses that looked like they had been cut from the bottoms of two Coca Cola bottles. He had a dreamy smile on his face, and hummed softly as he read, yumpa-pumpa-pum.

He looked up triumphantly. "Okay, I know just where this is, so you come with me now, yes? I take your bag to my cab, yes? The fare is 80 shekels, yes? Where is the bag? Here, yes? Okay, let's go!" He stopped talking long enough to reach for David's suitcase.

"Wrong!" boomed David as he sat down astride the suitcase before the little man could lift it off the ground. The cabbie let go of the handle and stared at him. A small crowd started to gather, amused by the confrontation. David looked the cabbie in the eye and smiled his own little smile. David might be a kid, but he was a New York kid. He had been beating off hustlers since he was ten years old, old enough to take the train into the City from Oceanside by himself. He had seen a thousand guys try to put the bite on the upstate yokels. David didn't play sucker, not in the City, and not in Israel, either.

"My friend," David continued, "I think we should start over. This is what we're going to do. You're going to pick up this suitcase and walk with me over to the information booth. Then I'm going to ask the nice lady how much the cab fare ought to be. Now, you said 80 shekels, which means that a very high price would be 20 shekels. The lady will tell me that the fare ought to be about 12 shekels, and then you'll say that with the traffic today, it will be more, so we'll agree on 15 shekels, right? Now, shall we go through that little charade, or do you want to just agree on a 15 shekel fare right now so we can get going?" David got off the suitcase and stood next to it, waiting. The cabbie shrugged and picked up David's bag. The little crowd broke up, laughing. A few people even applauded.

Five minutes later, David was sitting in the back seat of the cab, wondering whether he had been so smart after all. He had never seen such driving! The cab's speedometer was broken, so he couldn't tell for sure how fast they were going, but it felt like about 80 miles an hour. The driver, whose name turned out to be Yankel, seemed to keep the accelerator pinned to the floor at all times. Whenever they overtook a vehicle, Yankel would begin shouting something incomprehensible in Hebrew, jam his hand down on the horn button, and continue to shout as they swerved around the car ahead without slackening speed at all. Then Yankel would release the horn, stop shouting, turn completely around and smile insanely at David for an interminable ten seconds. Then he would turn and face forward until the next vehicle loomed up ahead. David never saw him touch the brake pedal. Furthermore, it looked to David as if every other car, bus, and truck on the road also used exactly the same method of locomotion. David had never thought it possible, but he found himself thinking "This is worse than New York!"

Forty endless minutes later, the cab drew up in front of a nondescript apartment block in the New City, the western part of Jerusalem. Its rough concrete facade reminded David of a low income housing project in the Bronx. Yankel heaved himself out of the driver's seat, waddled around to the back of the cab, and popped the trunk. David jumped out of the cab and walked around to the trunk, too. He reached into his pocket, and pulled out the wad of unfamiliar banknotes. "You want some help counting the fare, yes?" Yankel piped up, though without much hope. David snorted a laugh, carefully counted out the fare, handed it to Yankel and stuffed his remaining bankroll back deep into his pants pocket. David reached into the trunk to get the enormous suitcase, reconciled to pulling his back out, when Yankel reached past him, heaved the bag out like it was weightless, and carried it into the building and up three flights of stairs as David panted along behind him. They strode along a dimly lit corridor floored with tan and brown asphalt tile, then stopped abruptly in front of an anonymous green door. Yankel dropped the suitcase on the ground, then turned to David. "You're OK for an American, kid. Have a good visit, yes?" Then he turned and disappeared down the hall. David watched him go, smiled to himself, shook his head, then reached up and pushed the doorbell.

David could hear the thunder of bare baby feet pounding across the floor in response to the doorbell's strident buzz. There was the squeak of a faucet twisted suddenly off, then the lighter steps of an adult approaching the door. The security peephole in the door darkened momentarily, there was the rattle of a chain being unfastened, the click of the door latch, and then David was looking into the smiling face of Sid Goldman's wife, Nina. He felt something grabbing at his calves, looked down, and saw two little blond kids' arms wrapped around his pants legs like vines. They giggled.

"David!" Cousin Nina gave him an enthusiastic hug, then stood back, grasped his shoulders and held him out at arm's length, her head tilted appraisingly to one side. "You look wonderful! Here, don't stand out there in the hall, come in, come in!" She switched to Hebrew and said something to the children, who giggled uproariously, let go of his legs, and scurried back into the apartment. David grabbed his suitcase and followed them in, shutting the door behind him. He lowered the suitcase carefully to the floor, then looked around.

The apartment was small, even by New York standards, and looked smaller than it actually was because of the profusion of baby paraphernalia that seemed to fill every available space. Standing in front of the worn green sofa were a double stroller and a playpen. Board books and little rubber blocks littered the floor. David could look along a minuscule corridor that connected the living room with two small bedrooms, one containing two cribs, the other a double bed and a single chest of drawers. The living room opened directly into the kitchen, whose center was almost completely taken up by a yellow metal table surrounded by six wooden chairs with cane seats. David stood by the front door, looking around uncertainly.

Cousin Nina caught his expression and smiled reassuringly. "Relax, David, there's always room for one more! You'll sleep on the couch, which is very comfortable, you'll eat at the table, and the rest of the time you'll be out of the apartment having adventures, chasing girls, doing who knows what. Everything will work out fine!" She walked over to the sink and started mixing something in a bowl. She turned to call over her shoulder "The bathroom is just next to our room, David.

Why don't you wash up, then come join me while I finish cooking. Your Cousin Sid will be home soon, we'll
make *shabbes*, and then we'll talk about getting you off
and running." She turned back to her work. As David
headed toward the bathroom, he couldn't help thinking
how nice it was to be with family, and what a wonderful,
relaxed vacation it was going to be.

June 19, 8:00 P.M. IDT   Jerusalem

The Israeli Army doesn't take any holidays, even the
ones dictated by God. They learned that lesson in the
Yom Kippur War, when the Arabs invaded on the holiest
day of the year and damned near won. In particular, the
Army doesn't rest on *shabbes*, Ten Commandments or
not. God is expected to understand.

Colonel Zvi ben-Aryeh had always taken the *shabbes*
shift. It was not that he was anti-religious. He had just
thought it was easier for him than for the men who had
families. Everyone had become used to it, so no one
thought it strange that he would spend the day alone in
the silent control station. Only this *shabbes* he was not
alone.

The rest of the skeleton crew had gone home in the
late afternoon, leaving Colonel ben-Aryeh sprawled
comfortably in the swivel chair in front of the master
status board. Sergeant Gradsteyn had been the last one
out, tossing the Colonel the master key and shambling
sloppily through the door. Then, a few hours later when
it had become completely dark, a few men, the right
men, had drifted back, one by one, until now they were
all here.

Avram Gush, the propellant man, was in his late for-
ties like the Colonel. He wore his black hair unfashion-
ably long and brushed to the side in a vain attempt to
hide the fact that it was beginning to thin on top. He sat
easily on the edge of a plotting table, one leg resting on
the ground to take most of his weight, the other pulled
up so that his knee was supported while the rest of the
leg dangled over the edge. He had lost both his sons in
the Lebanon campaign and three grandchildren in a
grenade attack on a schoolbus.

Shimon Naphtali, the guidance system technician,
stalked around the room. He nervously picked up pen-
cils, pens, whatever he could reach, toyed with each
object for an uncomfortable moment, and then abruptly
replaced it in its original position. He had been a boy in
his early twenties when his bride of six months had had
a shrapnel hysterectomy. He was still in his early twenties, but he was no longer a boy.

Jonah Frischman, the warhead specialist, had a
neatly trimmed salt and pepper beard and the tanned
open face of the farmer he had once been. Jonah had
given up farming and family life when a rocket fired
from the Golan Heights slammed into the kibbutz nurs-
ery during his wife's shift. He sat stolidly in a swivel
chair next to Colonel ben-Aryeh's and waited for things
to begin.

Menachem Aronot, the silo mechanic, was the old
man of the group. He stood quietly in front of the status
board, examining the pattern of lights. The green bulbs
reminded him of the lights on the machine that kept
alive the little that was left of his wife. He saw little green
lights glowing every day during his visit to the nursing
home as he looked down at the insensate ruin of her

that the terrorist's bomb hidden in the vegetable bin at the supermarket had left. He leaned slightly to the right to take some of the weight off the artificial leg that had been the bomber's legacy to him.

Ben-Aryeh started softly.

"We're here because the idiot politicians are getting ready to march us into the gas chambers again. They want to give up the Golan, so the Syrians can shell us at their leisure. They say that the Arab states will push Hezbollah out of southern Lebanon. Hezbollah will leave Lebanon when pigs fly. They say that the Arabs will sign a peace treaty. A peace treaty is a worthless piece of paper. They say that the Palestinians will have a state, but no one will give them arms. They will only give them small arms for police purposes. The Palestinians are already killing us with their police weapons. And when they have their own state, they will get all the arms they want, because they will be the ones guarding the border. The fox will be guarding the henhouse.

"And besides giving them all that land, what do we do? We give those murderous bastards more tools to kill us with! We give them electronic technology, which they will put into missile guidance systems so they can blow our wives and parents to bits. We give them biological technology to use to make the weapons for biological warfare, so we can watch our children choke out their last breaths in agony. We give them trade to make money to buy more guns to kill us with. We open our borders so their killers can come freely into Israel.

"And it will never stop as long as we allow Islam to exist! When the Romans cut out the heart of Judaism by destroying the Temple in Jerusalem, it took us nineteen-hundred years to regain the courage to found our own country again. We can do the same to the countries of Islam! It is time for us to cut out their heart! It is time for us to destroy Mecca!"

Colonel ben-Aryeh looked around the room at the grim faces, ranging from pinkly boyish to greyly bearded, but all with a common hardness, the hardness that comes from the unceasing contemplation of gnawing, unending, irretrievable loss. He had chosen them carefully. Propulsion, guidance, weapon, and launcher are the technical elements needed to deliver a nuclear strike. Anger, pain, grief, and bitterness are the emotional elements needed to achieve the same goal. Now, thought Colonel ben-Aryeh, now it begins. Vengeance is mine, saith the Lord. Maybe so. But some of it is mine, too.

June 20, 10:30 A.M . EDT   New York
Even in the heat of June, the Sunday morning joggers thud along the Long Island sidewalks like a herd of obese antelope. Reeboks and Avias pounded the pavement. Sam Hirsch hated it, but that damned Dr. Brownstein had an obsession about jogging, and Sam's wife Barbara had an obsession about Dr. Brownstein. "You listen to Dr. Brownstein, Sam, you do what he says! Exercise and more exercise, an aspirin every other day, and you'll live forever! Or longer! Keep sitting around on your fat *tuchis*, and it's curtains!" Yeah, right, sure, thought Sam, gritting his teeth, glancing wryly at the brightly colored Nike swoosh logo on the chest of his sweat-soaked running suit. Unless I die of pneumonia or some other damn disease I get from exhausting myself.

Sam took the final turn and headed south down Frederick Street toward home. In spite of himself, he felt a hint of pleasure in being on the home stretch, and actually kicked in a final burst of speed up the front steps as he saw Barbara watching him from the living room window. He turned the unlocked knob of the front door, walked into the mud room, kicked off his running shoes, and ran upstairs for a quick shower.

Ten minutes later, Sam trotted downstairs in his usual Sunday wardrobe of golf shirt, double-knit slacks, and brown canvas crepe soled shoes. He walked across the pale green shag wall-to-wall that Barbara had selected for the living room *and* the entrance hall *and* the dining room, pulled out the armchair at the head of the Williamsburg reproduction dining room table, and settled down with a contented sigh to undoing all the benefits of his exercise program with a world-class dose of salt and cholesterol cleverly concealed in a lox and cream cheese filled bagel. Barbara and the kids had already started filling their plates with smoked fish and sliced cheeses. As Sam joined in the happy chatter around the table, he thought as he always did on Sunday morning how amazingly comfortable life in suburban America had become for this generation.

The table talk was momentarily interrupted by the chime of the doorbell playing the first few bars of the "William Tell Overture," another one of Barbara's decorating masterstrokes. "Aaron, will you get the door, please?" said Sam, not too hopefully. Surprisingly, Aaron got up with only perfunctory *boorching*, muttered complaining, that abruptly cut off when he opened the door to see his grandfather standing on the step. "So, *boychik*" said his grandfather, "are you going to stand there in the middle of the doorway like a linebacker all day or are you going to let me in?" Aaron laughed and stepped aside.

The old man strode in briskly, removed his black snap-brimmed hat, hung it on the brass coat rack, and proceeded into the dining room. He walked quickly around the table, kissing brusquely as he went, then pulled up a chair and sat down. Barbara was out of her chair like a racehorse bursting from the starting gate, filling his plate, pouring his coffee, fussing effusively. With all her faults, Barbara Feldstein Hirsch knew how to treat her husband's father.

Between tremendous bites of herring and bagel, Izzie Hirsch conducted a general interrogation of Aaron and his sister Sarah, while Sam and Barbara watched with tolerant amusement. Sarah was just getting launched into a dissertation on her latest roller-blading accomplishments when the phone rang. Barbara glanced at the gold Rolex she always wore, even in the shower. It showed exactly eleven o'clock. Her face lit up and she bounded into the kitchen, almost squealing "It must be David!" The rest of the family exploded away from the table throughout the house, diving for extensions.

David's voice was amazingly clear, considering the maze of satellite links, underground cables, switches, relays, and overhead wires it had had to go through to get from Jerusalem to Oceanside. "Hi Mom, hi Dad, hi monsters!" came crisply over the handsets, to be answered with a cacophony of replies from everyone at once. Communications broke down until Barbara unleashed a tremendous *geschrei*, a shriek of "*Shah*! Everybody shut up except David and me! Everybody will get a turn." She waited for a satisfactory silence, then continued "So, David, say hello to your grandfather — he's on the line, too. Then tell us what you've been doing." David's smile was almost audible. "Hi, Zayde! Everything's terrific. Sid and Nina are really being wonderful to me. I spent today just walking around the city. It's unbelievable! All the places you read about in books — they're real! And I'm starting to meet all kinds of people. When I finish making this phone call, I'm going back to Cousin Sid's for dinner. They've invited some friends over to meet me."

Barbara Hirsch was a direct woman. She was delighted that her son was enjoying himself, absorbing some culture, but that wasn't why she wanted him in Israel this summer. "That's terrific, David," she answered, "but, tell me, are you meeting any girls? *Jewish* girls?" On their respective extensions in the entrance hall and the master bedroom, Sam and his father simultaneously mumbled "*Oi!*" But David didn't seem to get his back up. After a momentary hesitation, he said "Well, sure, Mom, the people coming over tonight have a daughter my age. But I'm not looking for anybody, you know. I've got someone already." Barbara's voice oozed sugar. "Of course, darling, I know that. Look, I've monopolized the conversation long enough. Talk to your father."

The conversation wound quickly through the rest of the family, and in twenty minutes it was done. As the family reassembled in the living room, Barbara looked like she had swallowed a canary. Sam gave her a mildly dirty look. Barbara was having none of it. "Don't look at me in that tone of voice, Sam" she said, flopping definitively into the brown Laz-E-Boy recliner next to the fireplace. "I wanted to find out, and I did find out. He doesn't have to be looking to find somebody. Maybe that somebody will find him. The point is, he isn't around *her*!"

CHAPTER 5

July 10, 6:00 P.M. EEST   *Tyre, Lebanon*

On the patio of his home on a hilltop on the outskirts of Tyre, Mahmoud Mahdin sat comfortably at the head of the teak table, digesting his dinner of hummus, tabouli, grilled lamb, and some grapes for dessert. The grapes were superb. He had brought them home from the shipment his company had received today from the Bekaa Valley, the agricultural heart of Lebanon, which you wouldn't know from the newspapers. To the press, the Bekaa Valley was just a haven for terrorists. What a shame! A light breeze kept the patio deliciously cool, and he was enjoying looking out over the city. Mahmoud's wife Amira was seated at his left, a look of concern on her face. The younger children had finished eating and were playing quietly in the next room, so she could talk freely.

"Mahmoud, I am worried about Jasmine. I am worried about her choice of friends, male friends, in particular. She is becoming infatuated with a *Yihud*." Mahmoud sighed. Amira was wilting under the constant onslaught of anti-Jewish propaganda that dominated the press, magazines, and television. And, as she aged, she was turning ever more inward, back to her roots. But Lebanon was not Saudi Arabia, praise Allah, with women isolated, enslaved almost. Being obsessed with the religious persuasion of Jasmine's friends was a waste of time. He remembered an earlier Lebanon, when he was a boy, when ethnic friction was not much of an issue. Now, with a civil war not so many years ago, and continued fighting with the Israelis, and craziness on the Syrian border, it seemed that ethnicity was everything. But Jasmine was far away from all that now, studying in America. Mahmoud couldn't see the harm in her liking a Jew, at least during her stay in America. It wasn't as if she was planning to marry him. But you do not treat your wife with disrespect in a country as Westernized as Lebanon. Plus, fighting with Amira always made him feel ill, much more so lately, with his recurring head-aches. So he was moderate in his response.

"I understand your feelings, Amira. But Jasmine is an intelligent woman. She would not be spending time with an evil person. Not all Jews are evil, despite the propaganda."

Amira was not placated. "That's all well and good, Mahmoud, but Jasmine is reaching marriageable age. She's a good girl, I am not worried about her morals. But it is time for her to think about having a family, and she doesn't need to develop a habit of keeping company with boys who are not Muslims. We don't need a Jew in the family! And those Jews are stubborn, her friend would never say the *Shahadah* and convert to Islam. We need to make an end of this. Either she stops spending time with this *Yihud*, or we are bringing her back home!"

Mahmoud could feel his blood pressure rising. His head began to hurt again, really hurt this time. He would not tolerate Amira threatening to ruin his daughter's life. He prided himself on always maintaining a calm demeanor, but this was a special case. Jasmine was special. He jumped up from the table and shouted "We will do no such thing, Amira! Jasmine has a wonderful opportunity, and she earned it by years of hard work! She is at a fine university, one we could never afford to send her to if she hadn't earned a scholarship. She will finish her studies without interruption! Now shut up! I will listen to no more of your bigoted idiocy." The pain in his head increased. He sat down heavily on the floor. Amira rushed to his side. "Mahmoud, what is it? Are you sick?" He tried to answer, but the words wouldn't come. He fell onto his side, and the world turned black.

July 10, 4:25 P.M. EDT   **New York**

A college dormitory is a depressing place during summer vacation, empty except for a few berserkly dedicated writers of theses and a handful of foreign students. Nevertheless, Jasmine Mahdin was happy as she answered her cell phone and recognized her mother's number. It was always so nice to hear from home, even if a little bit surprising considering how recently she had received the last call. But this time, she was not ready for it.

She listened unbelievingly. Her left hand went involuntarily to her mouth, stifling the scream of denial that rose within her. She sat rigidly on the wooden seat of the tubing-framed desk chair, her breath coming in shallow, desperate gasps. She stammered "Yes, I'll be there right away," and hung up. Then, as the minutes passed, her breathing slowed and she began to cry.

How unfair, how terribly, bitterly, unreasonably unfair of God to strike at her father, her wise, kind, loving father! Mahmoud Mahdin was a man of faith, a man of strength, a man of compassion. Even in the chaotic hell of Lebanon, where you never knew whether the bullet that was going to kill you would come from a Christian, a Muslim, or an Israeli gun, he had managed somehow to keep the family together, to make the family vegetable business prosper, to find the money for Jasmine to travel to America to study. And after all that, to have his body fail him! A cerebral aneurism, something exploding in his brain. Yet, it could have been worse. At least he was still alive.

Jasmine went over the conversation in her mind. "There is nothing to be done for your father here. If he is to have any chance, he needs what the doctors tell us is unbelievably complicated surgery. Many people love your father, Jasmine, and even in this war-cursed world, there are still some kind hearts on all sides. The only place that your father can be helped is Occupied Palestine and, Allah be praised, the doctors at the Hadassah Hospital in Jerusalem have agreed to treat him. But there is great risk, great, great risk. It would strengthen him so much to see you, and he will need all the strength he can get. You must come to him in Jerusalem, before the operation is attempted. The Israeli authorities have agreed to allow us all to enter. Hurry, Jasmine, and Allah be with you on your journey."

Still crying, Jasmine Mahdin stood and walked over to the wardrobe that occupied the wall next to her bed. She stood on her toes to reach the soft canvas travelling bag stored on the top shelf. She pulled the bag down, brushed off the dust, unzipped it and threw it on the bed. Hurriedly, she began to pack.

July 11, 9:25 P.M . IDT   **Jerusalem**

The corridor outside the neurosurgery unit operating theater on the seventh floor of the Main Building on the Ein Kerem campus of Hadassah Hospital smells like hospital corridors everywhere. No amount of scrubbing ever gets rid of the effluvia of fear and hope that its occupants somehow leave behind after hours, or days, or weeks or months or years of waiting tensely on the padded vinyl chairs. Maybe they secrete adrenalin in their sweat.

Jasmine Mahdin sat next to her mother, holding her mother's hand tightly in both of hers. They made an odd couple, Jasmine still in her Western student's travelling outfit of jeans and sweatshirt, her mother in a somber black dress which, while Western, still harked back to traditional garb. She looks so frightened, thought Jasmine, and it is so unlike her to dress this way. But at a time like this, I suppose she draws strength from the tradition. And from me. How strange, she thought, how very strange to be the donor of strength instead of the recipient. All my life, I have been a child taking spiritual nourishment and have been able to give back so little. I'm glad I can give back something now. She caressed her mother's hand gently, and whispered "Allah protects us all, my mother. It will be all right." She felt an answering pressure, leaned her head back against the wall, and closed her eyes. Please let it be all right, she prayed, please.

The silence of the corridor was suddenly broken by the slam of the operating theater doors against the wall. Jasmine looked up to see two doctors walking toward her, gauze masks untied and hanging casually down across the fronts of their green surgical scrub shirts. The bulky white cloth booties worn in the operating room to prevent static electricity that might cause the anesthetic to explode made almost no sound as they scuffed along the floor. Jasmine tried desperately to read their faces, but all she could detect was emotional and physical exhaustion. They had been in there for nine and a half hours.

"Mrs. Mahdin?" Almost unconsciously, Jasmine and her mother rose together to face the doctors, like prisoners awaiting a verdict. The older doctor of the pair was speaking Arabic with a heavy Israeli accent. His face was lined like a peach pit, and his eyebrows beneath the surgical cap were bushy and grey and focused attention on his huge nose, hooked like the beak of a bird of prey. It should have been a frightening face, and yet the voice conveyed a warmth and compassion that took the sting out of the harsh features. His accent made him difficult to understand, and it was fully a minute before Jasmine could be sure that he was giving them good news. She turned to her mother and embraced her with relief. Praise be to Allah, her father would be all right! There was still some justice in the world!

It was with difficulty that Jasmine brought her attention back to the doctor's continuing speech. "Your husband will be convalescent for several weeks, Mrs. Mahdin, but there are a number of things you can do to speed his recovery. What I'd like to do now is turn you over to my associate, who is the specialist in post-operative care for patients who have gone through surgery like this. Besides," he smiled, "his Arabic is much, much better than mine." Jasmine half turned to the right to face the younger doctor. He was a slight, middle-aged man with wire-rimmed glasses. Jasmine noticed that he wore a heavy stainless steel chronograph on his left wrist. "Hello" said Hussein Musawi.

July 15, 9:00 A.M. EDT Washington, D.C.

Achmed Zarah, Executive Director of the Council on American Islamic Relations sat in the reception hall of the Saudi Arabian Embassy in Washington, fidgeting in the leather armchair as he gazed up at the portrait of King Yamani above the receptionist's desk. Zarah had a neatly trimmed moustache and goatee, and wore wrap-around black Prada glasses with tinted lenses. He was dressed conservatively in a navy pinstriped Brooks Brothers suit, white shirt, and a red tie with small white polka dots. He looked just like every other lawyer, lobbyist, and politician that infested the city. But he wasn't.

The drive all the way across the city from CAIR headquarters in the plebian southeast quadrant of the city to Embassy Row in the northwest had been tiresome, the usual game of dodg'em with taxis driven by Asian engineering students reading open textbooks on their front seats. He had been afraid that he would be late for the meeting. And one did not want to keep the Minister of Defense of the Kingdom of Saudi Arabia waiting.

The young male receptionist answered the buzzing phone on his desk, listened for a moment, hung up and said "The Prince will see you now." He beckoned to a page standing quietly against the wall, and Zarah was escorted to an elevator that whisked him and his minder to a small conference room on the top floor. The page's discreet knock on the door was greeted by a barked "Come in!" The page opened the door, took a step back and waved Zarah into the room.

Prince Salman was seated on a black Aeron chair at a small round walnut table, facing the door. He pointed to the similar chair directly across the table and said "Sit!" As soon as Zarah had settled himself, the Prince continued "To begin with, let me remind you that this meeting never happened. I am not in Washington, and you have never met me. Should word of this meeting leak out, something highly unpleasant will happen to you and your family. Do you understand?" Zarah nodded silently. The Prince continued "Now, on to business. You have been summoned here because we need to deliver an informal message to the American public.

"There are great changes in the worldwide balance of power that are about to occur, and very soon we will no longer be forced to issue only weak protests when the mass media of the infidels malign Islam. We do not want our strengthened posture to provoke a war with the United States, a country full of anti-Islamic hotheads, at least not yet. But remember, the anti-Islamists are that way for one reason – they fear us. It is necessary to increase that fear until it paralyzes them. We need them to be incapable of action by the time that the new developments occur.

"The most rabid of the infidels, who have a disproportionate impact on the public debate, are the swine who listen to talk radio, the participants in the political blogosphere. We must begin driving them into a state of total cowardice.

"You are to immediately initiate an anonymous national call-in campaign to the programs of the Rush Limbaughs and the Michael Grahams of the talk radio sphere. You will provide callers in every radio market serving more than one-hundred thousand listeners. You will make these calls from disposable cellphones. You will expand your monitoring of the major political websites, and provide correspondents to saturate their comment sections. We will provide you with web portals that will obliterate any trace of the origin of your messages before forwarding them to your targets. Our financial support provides you with funding more than adequate for this purpose.

"And all the messages will have the same theme: temper your language or face dire consequences."

July 18, 8:00 A.M. IDT   *Jerusalem*

Hussein Musawi slammed his cell phone shut angrily and muttered an obscenity under his breath. An orderly walking along the corridor gave him a faintly reproving look, despite the fact that Musawi's surgical greens clearly outranked bedpan-handler's blue. Rank doesn't cut much ice in Israel. Musawi shook his head in annoyance and walked off down the corridor. He turned left at the first junction and walked into the staff coffee room, where he grabbed a cup of strong coffee, dumped in six teaspoons of sugar, and sat down at an isolated table in one corner.

He stirred the coffee slowly, relishing the resistance that the syrupy mixture presented to the spoon. He always drank mint tea, but this was a special situation. Coffee, made the sugary sweet Arab way, was balm to the tongue and the stomach, nothing like the bitter, watery camel piss Europeans called coffee and the cursed Jews were always swilling down in huge gulps. He took a tiny sip, rolled it around on the tip of his tongue, and let it slide smoothly down his throat. Smoothness, that was the trick, that was the secret of Arab success. He frowned. He certainly would need it now. That had been a very bad phone call. There was a problem.

Why hadn't Mustafa's accursed sister watched where she was stepping? Couldn't she recognize a simple pressure mine? Now she was stuck north of the Lebanese border, lying in a hospital with her left leg patched together with catgut and plaster, instead of riding peacefully south on the old bus, the plastic explosive sitting discretely invisible inside the melons in her string bag. Praise be to Allah that she hadn't picked them up before the explosion. They were still ready to be sent. But who was he going to get for a pack animal? Mustafa's sister had been perfect. She could pass through the border without making even a ripple with that World Health Organization passport of hers. Now, it would take something else.

Hussein Musawi glanced across the room at a small knot of OR nurses chatting easily together. So much medicine for such a tiny country, he thought. These Jews worship medicine more than they do God. So let us exploit that obsession. Let us kill them with curing. Abruptly, he rose from the table. He had it.

He walked quickly out of the coffee room, pulled out his cell phone, and made a brief call. Then he continued to the corridor outside the room where Jasmine Mahdin and her mother sat quietly watching her father sleep. He caught Jasmine's eye and beckoned her out to join him. He pushed his features into an expression of mild concern, not enough to terrify, just enough to guarantee her attention. "Miss Mahdin," he said, "I need your assistance. I am a little concerned with the pace of your father's recovery." He watched with satisfaction as the corners of her mouth drew tight. "As you know, your father's blood type is rather rare, and we pretty well exhausted the hospital's supply during the surgery. So, just as a precaution, I want to be sure we have enough on hand. I have managed to locate an adequate supply and to get permission to have it shipped here. There is, however, a small problem." He paused just long enough for Jasmine to turn slightly pale and begin to breathe just a little too rapidly. Then he continued. "The blood is in a UN field hospital just north of the Lebanese border in the security zone, and they are insisting that we send up a ton of paperwork before they release it for shipment. If I just put the paperwork into the blood bank exchange system, it will take weeks to get through the bureaucracy. And weeks could be too long." He shook his head slowly from side to side. Jasmine turned paler. "So," he continued decisively, Great Healer act in full flood, "I need someone to hand carry the papers to Lebanon and bring back the blood. Everything would go much more smoothly at the border if the courier had a Lebanese passport. Could you possibly....?" His voice trailed off.

Jasmine felt a cold knot forming in the pit of her stomach. Southern Lebanon! She closed her eyes for a moment, and the blank screen of her eyelids was covered with a horror movie of blood and smoke and bodies. Then she opened her eyes and looked back into the room at her father, his chest rising and falling rapidly, a grey stubble making his face look old, old. What choice did she have? "Of course I'll go," she murmured.

Hussein Musawi nodded sympathetically. "Excellent! And don't worry, it's not nearly as bad as the papers say. You can catch a bus tomorrow morning around ten up to Netanya. I can arrange for a UN shuttle to pick you up at the central bus station, bring you to the hospital, and return you for the bus ride back. By tomorrow night you'll be with your father again." Jasmine smiled uneasily at him. He smiled back, then looked down with what seemed to be slight embarrassment. He started to speak, then hesitated uncertainly. "Is there something else?" Jasmine asked, trying to make it easier for him. He shifted his weight uncertainly back and forth from one foot to another, then blurted it out like a little boy. "Well, yes there is. You know, Lebanon is famous for sun melons. They're very hard to find here in Jerusalem. My friend at the hospital has bundled up a bag of them for me. On your way back, could you do me a personal favor? Could you perhaps bring back my bag of melons?" He had done it perfectly. Jasmine's motherly assent was classic. Hussein Musawi smiled.

July 18, 10:00 A.M. IDT   Near Netanya

David Hirsch swayed violently in his seat as the big green Egged bus with the huge white X on the side veered around yet another fender bender, then whipped back into the right lane of the coastal highway, heading north along the Mediterranean toward the town of Netanya. The wild ride didn't seem to bother his cousin Sid at all. He just slumped easily on the blue cloth seat, arms folded across his chest, his eyes occasionally closing as he drifted in and out of a doze. His eyes flicked open again as David let out an involuntary whoop. "Still not used to the driving, I see." Sid wriggled erect in his seat. "Well, you might try closing your eyes. That's what the drivers do," he deadpanned. David had to laugh.

The bus was fairly crowded, half with soldiers on their way to new postings in the north, half with assorted civilians. The soldiers looked distinctly unmilitary to David, despite their uniforms, compared to the tautly turned out military people he saw travelling in the States. There, travelling soldiers were all spit and polish, shiny black shoes, crisply pressed tunics, rows of decorations. Here, it was khaki duffel bags thrown crazily across the seats, shirts untidily open halfway down the chest, and Uzis leaning sloppily against the windows. Even the officers, like Sid, had a casual informality about them that didn't fit in very well with David's vision of military discipline.

David turned away from the window to take advantage of Sid's waking period. "Sid, really, how did you manage to get away so you could come with me to Netanya? I really appreciate the company, but I hate to complicate your life." "I *like* a complicated life," Sid replied. "That's why I live in this crazy country! But, in fact, I had to get up to a facility near Netanya tomorrow to take care of some Army business anyway. So, actually, you're doing me a favor by keeping *me* company. It's a *shlepp* and a half dragging up here alone." Sid squirmed in his seat, then stretched his arms over his head and yawned. Just thinking about the trip had triggered his conditioned boredom reflex. To get his mind off it, Sid continued "How much do you know about Netanya?" David shrugged. "Nothing, really, beyond the fact that it's the diamond cutting capital of the world. Dad just told me to introduce myself to Mr. Abramowitz at The Shamir Diamond Company. I've got a meeting with him tomorrow. I'm supposed to carry a shipment home when I leave." His mouth twisted in embarrassment. "It makes my trip tax-deductible." Sid caught the expression and chuckled. "That sounds like Uncle Sammy. Well, don't worry kid, I won't tell the IRS about your side trips. Your secret's safe with me. And you'll like Netanya. Never mind the diamonds. What matters for a guy your age is that Netanya's got a terrific beach with plenty of girls. Unless you go too far north; then you hit the *frumme*, the very Orthodox beach at Qiryat Sanz where a man can't even sit on the sand when women are around."

Sid's lecture on the wonders of Israeli beach etiquette was abruptly cut off by the sudden screech of the brakes. David looked forward through the windshield and saw that an unmarked white panel truck had skidded through a ninety degree turn and come to rest blocking both lanes of the highway. Three white-shirted men were milling about the vehicle and looking under its open hood. He was surprised to see that the soldiers, who had greeted the earlier wild careening of the bus with sleepy indifference, were suddenly extremely alert. In seconds, the apparently randomly stacked guns had been grabbed by their owners, the slides racked, and swung into alert position. As the bus shuddered to a stop about twenty yards in front of the stalled truck, he turned to see Sid jump out of his seat and hurry forward, taking time only to bark "Stay where you are, David!" David saw Sid hurriedly snapping orders to the other soldiers and then the scene in front of the bus shifted from amusing chaos to terrifying menace. As the bus sighed into immobility, the men around the truck suddenly ducked behind it.

They reappeared seconds later brandishing AK47 assault rifles, dived onto the road, and began firing wildly at the bus.

David found himself lying face down on the floor without remembering how he had gotten there, hands crossed protectively over the back of his head to ward off the shards of flying glass from the splintering windows. He smelled smoke, and as he risked a quick glance at the front of the bus, he saw flames beginning to peep out from the floor next to the driver's seat. Someone had managed to open the emergency door at the back, and he crawled toward it, hoping that he would make it out before the gas tank went up. He slid through the opening and did a somersault onto the road surface, then continued rolling off the road and into a culvert. As he caught his breath, he saw that the rest of the passengers had ended up in the same place. The soldiers had taken up positions at either end of the group of civilians, and were firing back at the terrorists, who had retreated behind their truck. He heard a dull boom from the road and peeked over the lip of the culvert to see the remains of the bus explode into flame. My God, he thought sickly, I wonder if anybody was still in there. His thought was cut off as he was pulled back under cover by a soldier on his right, who repeated "Head down! Head down!" and then something in Hebrew. David's Hebrew wasn't too good, but he recognized *m'tumtam*, the word for "idiot."

David looked around to try to find Sid and saw that all but two of the soldiers were working their way along the culvert to his left in the direction of the truck. The two remaining soldiers continued exchanging fire with the terrorists. As the assault group came up parallel with the truck, David saw them suddenly swarm over the edge of the culvert and blanket the area behind the truck with bullets. He wasn't expecting to hear a cry of agony to his right. He turned away from the firefight to find a soldier sprawled on the ground clutching his side. David looked beyond him to see that one of the terrorists had apparently separated from the others and had worked his way behind the group from the bus. As David watched, he saw the man reach into his pocket and pull out a grenade.

There wasn't a lot of time. Desperately, David looked around for a weapon he could use. The wounded soldier's Uzi was an incomprehensible madhouse of safeties and autofire switches. But the big pistol on his hip was something David understood. David dived for the holster on the wounded man's side, ripped out the big pistol, racked the slide, and emptied the magazine into the terrorist's chest before he could even pull the grenade's pin. He was still crouched on the bottom of the culvert, arms extended, elbows locked, squeezing the now impotent trigger over and over when he felt a hand on his shoulder and a familiar voice shouting "OK, David, OK, relax, it's all over." He looked up and saw Sid's dirt-streaked face staring wildly at him. David's breathing slowed. He dropped the now empty pistol onto the ground, and his hands began to shake. A wave of nausea overtook him, and he turned aside and vomited weakly onto the concrete. Then he sat down heavily, folded his arms across his knees and rested his head on them as he listened to the wail of an approaching ambulance. Sid sat next to him, an arm around his shoulders. Sid looked down at him with a mixture of affection and respect. "You know something, kid?" Sid said, "you're not a kid. Not at all. Where did you learn to handle yourself like that?"

Through the shock, David smiled and said "It's amazing what you can learn from your *zayde*. Truly amazing."

July 18, 2:00 P.M. IDT   Netanya

"Mom, please, try to calm down!" David Hirsch held the cell phone an inch away from his ear, half squinting his eyes to ward off the outraged shrieking that burst out of the earpiece. "Yes, Mom, sure, I know you're upset, but you don't have to worry. I'm perfectly fine. It's no worse than getting mugged in the City." That was the wrong thing to say. The squeaking from the earpiece got even louder and more raucous, its intensity undiminished by the twelve thousand miles of high technology linking Barbara Hirsch in Long Island with her son, standing in a secluded corner of the bus station in Netanya, Israel. Sid stood next to David, grinning at David's discomfiture. Finally, Sid took pity on him and wrenched the phone out of his hand. "Aunt Barbara, this is Sid," he said easily into the phone, his tone a honeyed elixir of reassurance. "Look, you have every reason to be upset. But it's all over now. And David's right...you ought to think of it as no worse than being mugged." The phone squawked again. Sid grimaced at David and shrugged. "Well, sure, Aunt Barbara, I understand that they don't usually mug you in New York with machine guns. Unless you're in the drug business." He winked at David, then continued "In any case, you ought to be awfully proud of your boy. David saved a lot of lives out there today. He's quite a kid. Quite a man, really. And this kind of thing doesn't happen here every day, you know, despite what you read in the American newspapers. The rest of David's stay will be quieter than it would be if he were back in New York. Lightning doesn't strike twice in the same place." Sid nodded encouragingly as the phone mumbled its grudging acceptance. "Really, don't worry, Aunt Barbara, we'll take good care of him. Love to everybody. Bye." Sid hung up the phone, puffed out his cheeks, and blew. "Come on, David, let's go" he said. "The trick to surviving when the threats never stop is to refuse to let that interfere with your life. We are going to sit down, have something to eat, check in to our motel, and go on just as we planned."

The Israeli authorities had been a lot more reasonable than the New York cops would have been in similar circumstances. In New York, he would have found himself in handcuffs lying face down on the back seat of a police car, and then spent three days in jail before things had started to be cleared up. Then he would have been indicted under the Sullivan Act and sued by the dead terrorist's family. Here, after fifteen minutes of questioning had rendered the situation only too clear, he had been patted on the back and sent off about his business. Successfully defending your life isn't a crime in Israel.

July 18, 6:00 P.M. IDT   **Jerusalem**

The little grey cat prowled happily around the dirt floor of the cellar, looking for something to eat. Finding nothing, it jumped onto Hussein Musawi's lap, curled up, and went to sleep. Musawi ignored it. He was busy listening unhappily to the news bulletin dribbling tinnily out of the tiny loudspeaker of the ancient radio. The mass of the building above and the dirt walls of the cellar cut out so much of the signal that the voice could barely be distinguished from the background cacophony of pops, gurgles, and static. But he could hear enough. He sat in his swivel chair, polishing his glasses carefully with a spotless linen handkerchief, his eyes apparently focused on this mundane task, but actually looking only inward. Around the rough wooden table, his fighters fidgeted uneasily. There were three fewer than there should have been. Musawi would demand a penance.

Without raising his eyes from his swirling fingers, Musawi began his whispered harangue. "Soldiers of Islam, we have suffered a grievous lapse in discipline. Three of our brothers have taken it upon themselves to violate the sanctity of our period of preparation. There can be no excuse for such disobedience. Drawing attention to ourselves can bring no benefit to our operation. The failure of their ill-conceived theatrics has resulted in their personal punishment. But there is yet another sin left unpunished."

For the first time, Musawi raised his eyes to confront his fighters. His fingers ceased their massaging of the lenses in their wire frames. His slightly out of focus pupils drifted slowly across their fearful faces. He blinked once, then continued "That sin is *your* sin. You knew! And yet, you neither stopped them nor informed me! You acted like children or women, giggling in anticipation, when you should have acted like men. And now, you cower in front of me like children again, guilty children with eyes averted dreading a just punishment, yet hoping for redemption through the suffering the punishment will bring. You are fools!" Musawi's voice rose slightly. To his men, it had all the impact of a hysterical shriek from anyone else. "Do you think there is time left to play at discipline? You are needed now, all your skill, all your devotion, not with minds clouded with pain. We are three fewer. That will make the task all the more difficult. Do you have any conception of what the streets will be like for the next six months? The roadblocks, the identity checks, the random arrests? If any one of you fails me again, in any way, by sin of omission or commission, I will simply kill him with no more thought than this." Musawi replaced his glasses and tucked his handkerchief into his shirt pocket. Then he reached down into his lap with his left hand and lifted the small grey cat onto the table. With his right, he drew the commando dagger from his belt. Grasping the hilt tightly in his fist, he plunged the blade down through the cat's neck, severing its spinal cord and pinning the corpse to the table. He released the knife and flicked the hilt with his forefinger. His mild expression had not changed. The knife vibrated gently, emitting a light thrum.

Hussein Musawi leaned back in the swivel chair, ignoring the slowly spreading pool of blood on the table. He was satisfied by the looks of revulsion that swept across the faces of his fighters. Killing the cat pointlessly would suffice. He continued, "The cat has now played the role of the ram in the story of the prophet Ishmael. He has taken the divine blow in your stead. And I will now tell you why I have been so generous. I have chosen the date for our act of *jihad*. It is a particularly appropriate one. It is a date that symbolizes the inevitable advance of the One True Faith across the whole of the globe. It is a date that for the eternal future will symbolize the rebirth of the Islamic purity of a liberated Palestine. Soldiers of Islam, we strike on the first day of Ramadan, the month of repentance! Now, the infidels ignore it. But our deed will burn that date into their calendar until the end of time!"

July 18, 6:00 P.M. IDT   **Jerusalem**

Colonel Zvi ben-Aryeh carefully closed and locked the door of his office. He drew the shade over the glass panel that looked out into the main control room. His privacy assured, he walked over to the classified filing cabinet, turned the knob of the combination lock, bent to open the bottom drawer, and extracted a tan file folder from the back section. It was the size of a sheet of legal paper. He straightened up, walked the two steps to his desk, and sat down with the file open in front of him, its outline sharp against the wooden surface under the intense light of the LED desk lamp.

Everything was coming together. Colonel ben-Aryeh flipped familiarly through the pages, reading everything, making occasional notations. Every detail was specified: the procedures for replacing the warhead activation device; for making the little wiring modifications that bypassed the various safety interlocks; for substituting the special ROM chip that altered the guidance cross-checks; for inactivating the emergency destruct system. It would take less than an hour to prepare the nuclear-tipped Sabra missile in Launch Complex 4 for its mission. It only remained to set the target coordinates and select the launch time.

Colonel ben-Aryeh reached into the folder and extracted a half-tone reproduction of a satellite photograph of a three acre square in the middle of Saudi Arabia. It was a photograph that any of a billion faithful

Muslims anywhere on the face of the planet would have recognized in an instant. It was a picture of the al-Haram Masjid, the great mosque of Mecca. In the center of the courtyard stood the *Kaaba*, the ancient stone cube that is the holy of holies of the faith of Islam, the destination of the throngs making the *haj*.

The photograph was overlaid with a tight coordinate grid, numbers printed on the periphery. Colonel ben-Aryeh leaned forward over the photograph. Carefully he located the *Kaaba*. Methodically, he read off its coordinates and transcribed them to an index card which he placed on the desk.

Turning slightly to his right, he opened the large side drawer and pulled out a calculator-sized chip programmer with a small keyboard and a microchip socket. He reached into his shirt pocket and took out a small plastic case containing an integrated circuit chip, removed the chip, and plugged it into the socket. As he tapped at the keyboard, the coordinates he had drawn from the satellite photograph were transcribed to the chip. He put the reprogrammed chip back in its case, returned the case to his pocket and put the programming device back in the drawer. When this chip had been installed in the missile, it would search single-mindedly for its new target. And it would find it.

Colonel ben-Aryeh felt a little dizzy as he contemplated the final step. No technology would come between him and his vengeance. He would push the button for the launch himself, feel his own hand strike the blow. And what a time he had chosen, what a just and proper time. It had come to him last week, as he read that silly article on the lunar calendar. It was strange that the Muslims relied on the moon for establishing their festivals, just as the Jews did. But the Muslims did not add leap-months, so that their holidays marched completely around the solar calendar every thirty-some odd years. Perhaps it was the hand of God that had arranged it; in any case, the perfect date would occur very soon. The date on which the world would be cleansed of Islam would be the first day of Ramadan, the month of fasting and repentance, a time to make amends for their sins. But true expiation requires suffering.

We will provide them with all the suffering they need.

CHAPTER 6

July 18, 2:15 P.M. IDT   *Netanya*

S id and David walked south along Gad Machnes Street, listening to the muted crash of waves breaking on the beach to their right. They paused to purchase *falafel*, chick pea fritters, served in a sandwich made of split flat bread filled with salad, from one of the ever-present street vendors. David was really hungry. With the boundless resilience of youth, he was practically recovered from the morning's events. The post-attack chaos of emergency vehicles, soldiers, police, and the inevitable news media had faded to a pale memory, interesting but no longer terrifying. It was a little harder to get rid of the thought that he had killed somebody. But, surprisingly, not a lot harder. The knowledge that he hadn't had any choice was an effective salve for his conscience. The fact that he hadn't had any personal contact with the man he had shot, either before or after the fact, lent the whole episode an aura of unreality. It was as if he had played a scene in a motion picture.

They sat down on a bench facing the beach. Sid finished his food, then leaned back and hooked his elbows over the back of the bench and stretched his legs out. David, who had gotten a double order, continued eating.

Sid stared at him in amusement. "If I ate like that after every fight, I'd weigh three hundred pounds! Then Nina would kick me out in the street." He looked fondly out across the beach. "You know, David, this is where I met her. It was right after I came to Israel, a kid fifteen months out of NYU. I had been living in a rathole in West Jerusalem, still sponging off my parents while I looked for something to do. Jobs weren't so easy to come by then, not that they are now, and I was taking advantage of the fact to justify playing beach bum for a few weeks. Everybody said how nice the Netanya beaches were, 'the Riviera of Israel,' so I decided to get a cheap motel room one weekend and check it out. It was pretty early in the season, not too many people on the beach. I was walking along feeling disappointed and thinking about heading for the next town, when I spotted this absolute bomb-shell in an infinitesimal bikini sitting all alone near the water. So I wandered over, sat down, and started to talk. My Hebrew was passable, and I always had a good line with the girls from the time I was twelve, so she started to talk to me. But it was something of a shock, because a girl who looked like that wasn't supposed to talk like that. There was no nonsense about her. As soon as she found out that I had made *aliyah*, immigrated, she started to grill me. Not about what I was going to do, but about why I had come. She was really pretty brutal, too, probing, prodding, suggesting all kinds of particularly embarrassing motives. My first reaction was to tell her to go to hell, but there was something there, an intensity of spirit, a challenge, that I just couldn't let pass. We ended up in my room, talking and making love for two days with almost no time out for sleep, and three weeks later we were married and I had joined the Israeli

Defense Forces." Sid sighed happily. "The best decisions are always the ones you make the fastest."

Sid stood abruptly and brushed the crumbs off the front of his trousers. "On which note," he continued, "I think we should take a walk around the town. Then I'm going to let you take off on your own while I check in at the motel, report to Jerusalem, and make some final preparations for my work tomorrow. Swing by the motel around eight and we'll grab some dinner." David hurriedly stuffed the last bite of his falafel into his mouth and jumped up to follow Sid down the street. "Sounds great," David mumbled around his mouthful.

July 19, 8:00 A.M . IDT   Near Netanya

The road was a featureless ribbon of concrete, a yellow line marking the diminutive shoulder which separated the road from the surrounding desert. All you could see from the road was an eight-foot cyclone fence topped with a mare's nest of concertina barbed wire surrounding a featureless concrete shed about ten feet square, with a parabolic radar dish and a radio antenna on the roof. The shed had no windows, and was just tall enough to accommodate a single steel door in the side, with no visible handle. Joined to the shed was a square concrete slab fifteen feet on a side and about three feet high, supporting a steel hemisphere with a seam running vertically all the way over the top. The rectangular sheet metal sign bolted to a gate in the fence blandly announced "Communications Relay Station 17." Who the hell that is supposed to fool, God only knows, Sid Goldman thought to himself, as he did every time he came here. It does as much good as the "Textile Mill" sign outside the Dimona nuclear plant that was a running joke with visiting American tourists, or the "Highway Department" sign he had heard the U.S. government put outside CIA headquarters in Langley, Virginia. Oh, well, he thought, maybe it fools the camels.

The soldier who had picked him up in Netanya wrenched the jeep to a stop in front of the gate and waited as a television pickup turned slowly to cover them. There was a soft whine as the lens unit rotated to bring them into focus, and both Sid and the driver reached into their shirt pockets and pulled out identification cards which they held up to the camera for inspection. A hollow voice boomed "Come on in, Sid" from a loud-speaker on a post just inside the gate. The Israeli army is highly disciplined, but it doesn't stand on ceremony. Addressing Captain Goldman as "Sid" was standard procedure. There was the grinding of an electric winch, the gate drew back, and the jeep growled quickly into Launch Complex 4. The winch ground again as the gate closed securely behind them.

Sid jumped lightly out the doorless side of the jeep and walked over to the shed, swinging an aluminum attaché case easily at his side. As he approached the door, a second television pickup swung to cover him. He again produced his identification, then waited as a series of thumps from behind the door played the accompaniment to the release of the electrically controlled locks. He looked over his shoulder at the driver, who was settling down behind the wheel of the jeep for a nap. The door swung open with a final click. Sid walked into the air-conditioned darkness and trotted down the narrow staircase into the gently humming subterranean semi-darkness of Silo Launch Control. It looked the way it always looked, a console with its battery of video screens and numeric readouts, and a bright red master arming switch in the center, its lock open and waiting for the insertion of the security key hanging around the neck of one of the authorized launch control officers. When the key was inserted and turned and the arming switch was thrown, the missile in Launch Complex 4 was ready to be sent on its way. The missile was topped with a 200 kiloton nuclear warhead, the nuclear warhead that Israel didn't have, of course.

Captain Yehudah Levin had turned away from the console to smile at Sid and give him a sloppy greeting, half wave, half salute. "How's the grand strategy business treating you, Sidney? Plan anything lately? Or do you still just carry ben-Aryeh's bags?" His dark face held an ironic half-smile. Captain Levin was a tactics and operations man at heart. He didn't have a lot of patience for staff officers, even Sid, and he went back a long way with Sid, all the way back to Lebanon in 2006. But the needle didn't bother Sid. He just wanted to get the job done and get home, so he merely answered "Yeah, that's right, Yehudah, I'm still just a *shlepper*. But at least I've got somebody better looking to spend time with than you do." Captain Mordechai Eytalon looked up from the communications desk in mock outrage. "Better looking than me? Wow!" He adjusted the black patch that covered the remains of his left eye socket with exaggerated vanity, then turned back to his screens. Everybody laughed, and Yehudah continued "No, really, Sid, what's new and exciting?" Sid paused for a moment, then responded "New? Nothing. Exciting? Well, I was on the bus that got shot up on the Netanya road yesterday morning. Exciting enough?"

The smiles dropped from the faces of the launch officers as if they had been slapped. Sid cut short the outburst of concern by saying "Look, I'm fine, but I'm a little tired, and I'd like to get done and get home as soon as possible. So let's get started, OK?" He walked over to the console and swung out a small metal stool that had been folded flat against the wall on its pivot post. He sat down on the stool, reached up and punched a numeric code into a keypad. As he finished, a panel swung down in front of him, forming a little desk and revealing a complex array of test jacks. Sid reached down, picked up his attaché case, and rested it on the little desk. He unsnapped the catches and raised the lid to reveal measuring instruments, their cables compactly stowed in a small compartment on the side. With a speed borne of long experience, he hooked the cables into the test jacks and began a long series of measurements.

Three hours later, Sid was done. The Sabra missile sitting ten feet in front of him beyond the wall was ready to go if, God forbid, it had to be used. The squat nuclear device sitting evilly in its nose was ready too. He was just pulling the last two cables out of the wall when he caught a snatch of mumbled conversation between Levin and Eytalon that didn't make a lot of sense. "How's that?" he asked as he quickly wrapped the cables into a compact ball and stowed them in the storage compartment. Levin glanced over, a slight flush of embarrassment darkening his face even more. "No harm meant, Sidney. I just said that I couldn't figure out what strange fascination Netanya holds for all you strategic types." Sid looked puzzled. "What fascination? Somebody gets out here once every three weeks. Big deal." Now it was Levin's turn to look puzzled. "Not this month, Sidney. In the last week we've had Gush out here poking around in the bird's motor, Naphtali screwing with the guidance system, Frischman tickling the warhead, and even old Aronot lubricating the silo doors. It's been like an Arab market." He chuckled nervously. "You'd think we were getting ready to go to war any second." His voice shifted to the slightly hostile tone of every front-line soldier trying to sort out what the brass actually has in mind. "What's really going on, Sid? You can let us in on it, can't you?"

Sid thoughtfully closed the testing set, got up, snapped the panel back into place, and swung his seat back against the wall. As he headed up the staircase, he gave the only answer he had. "I guess it's just a little extra dose of paranoia, Yehudah. Nothing to be concerned about. If I hear anything else, I'll let you know on the next trip." As he headed out the door and back to the jeep, he couldn't shake the feeling that something was not quite right. He had the primary responsibility for readiness inspections. So why hadn't he known about these special visits by all these technicians?

As Sid clambered back into the jeep, the driver snapped awake, hit the ignition switch, and headed back to the gate, which swung open with its usual grinding as they approached. Heading back down the road to Natanya, Sid casually asked the driver how he liked making all these runs out to the desert site. "Hell, sir," the corporal replied, "I don't mind at all. Once every three weeks isn't bad." Sid turned to look at the driver's face. It was relaxed and matter of fact. Sid turned forward again and stared down the road in thoughtful silence.

July 19, 9:00 A.M . IDT   **Netanya**

Maximillian Abramowitz was an Israeli by necessity but a Belgian by inclination. He sat behind his rosewood desk in the managing director's office of the Shamir Diamond Company, alternately pulling his white goatee and stroking his enormous moustaches as he looked curiously across the neat surface at David Hirsch. Even at the age of 88, he was still clearly the man in charge. "So you are the next generation of the House of Hirsch, hmm?" David decided that it was one of those questions that didn't need an answer; indeed Mr. Abramowitz didn't *want* an answer, so he fidgeted silently in the elegantly uncomfortable straight-backed visitor's chair while Mr. Abramowitz continued to look him over. He took advantage of the opportunity to look Mr. Abramowitz over right back. The president of Shamir Diamonds looked like Hercule Poirot's grandfather. He wore a dark brown suit; each of the few hairs on his head was held rigidly in place by some kind of hair dressing; and his fingernails were manicured like the White House lawn. David decided he looked completely out of place in Israel's casual society.

"So you think I look too stuffy for an Israeli, hmm?" Max Abramowitz squinted over the tops of his half glasses, a slight smile playing with the corners of his mouth. David couldn't help it — he started violently, almost falling off the chair. His hand sprang unconsciously to cover his mouth, in the fear that he had somehow involuntarily mumbled audibly what he had been thinking. David was not a rude guy.

"Well," Max Abramowitz continued with apparent satisfaction at David's reaction, "you're right. On the other hand, you don't look too much like a diamond merchant. So, let's agree that appearances can be deceiving, and don't mean very much anyway, and go on. Also, don't worry about your manners. You didn't say a thing. You didn't give me any funny look. I didn't read your mind. At my age, you know what everybody's thinking even without clairvoyance." He gave an old man's chuckle and leaned back in his high-backed desk chair, its supple cordovan leather rippling accommodatingly in response. "So, now, tell me, how are Izzie and Sam doing?"

David was grateful for an easy question. "Zayde and Dad are fine, Mr. Abramowitz." He launched into the standard visitor from afar litany, business is good, my brother and sister are well, my Mom sends her love, etcetera, ad nauseum. Max Abramowitz nodded genially through it all, hearing everything, at the same time trying to come to a judgment about the kid sitting in front of him who, the television had told him yesterday, had the guts and brains and, let's face it, the ferocity, to kill to prevent a mass murder. As David slowed to think of more trivia, Max Abramowitz asked it innocently. "Good, good, glad to hear it. And how was the bus ride up from Jerusalem?" He waited blandly for David's response, elbows resting on the polished surface of the desk, fingertips pressed together. David's face sobered. "I guess you didn't hear the news, Mr. Abramowitz. The bus ride wasn't so good. We were shot at by terrorists, and the bus driver and one of the passengers were killed. Luckily, there were a bunch of soldiers on the bus who got the terrorists before anyone else was hit." David shook his head unbelievingly, stood up, walked over to the window and stood looking out onto Herzl Street, his hands thrust deep into his pockets. "I was lucky to get out in one piece."

"Not lucky. Ready!" The old man was not smiling. "You got out in one piece, as you put it, because you shot that *momser*, that bastard, before he blew you to pieces. I watch the television, David, I know what happened. I just wanted to hear your version, and I'll give you some good advice. The next time you tell the story, don't be afraid to talk about what you did yourself." Max Abramowitz rose from his chair and walked around the desk and over to David. He held out his hand. "People don't often get a chance to meet a real hero, David. Never be so modest that you deny it to them. It's really all right to *kleb naches*, to take some satisfaction from your own actions. *Mazeltov!*" A little dazedly, David shook Max Abramowitz's hand.

The little man finished the handshake, then clapped his hands and rubbed them together briskly. "So!" he said, "now that we've introduced ourselves, let me show you the works. I'm very proud of it. It has taken over fifty years to get to this stage. But it's been worth it." They walked out of the managing director's office and down a narrow corridor with featureless walls that glowed a sickly yellow in the light of a single strip of industrial fluorescent lamps. The corridor terminated in a stainless steel door with a central locking wheel like the one David had seen on the safety deposit box vault at the downtown office of Citicorp. Max Abramowitz pushed a black button below a microphone grill mounted low on the wall at the level of *his* mouth and spoke a few words. There was a brief pause, and then the locking wheel in the center of the door spun counterclockwise and the door swung open smoothly on its massive hinges. Max

Abramowitz and David walked through the door and past an armed guard with a Sam Browne belt and an Uzi submachine gun into the heart of the international cut diamond industry.

Despite his age, Max Abramowitz bounced enthusiastically along down the aisles separating the rows of benches at which an army of artisans turned a river of misshapen rocks into a torrent of jewels. Although he had grown up in the business and had seen a few large stones in the process of being cut down, David had never seen a complete diamond factory before. He followed along with Max Abramowitz, watching with fascination as the cutters minutely adjusted the vises and jigs, then struck the bases of their chisels with weighted mallets to fracture the stones precisely along their natural cleavage planes. As they walked, Max Abramowitz happily regaled him with the history of the place.

"I came here from Brussels in 1939, David, before there was even a State of Israel. It was clear to me that Hitler was going to kill us all if we didn't get out." He paused, and his eyes looked far off into the past. Very quietly, he continued "It is still inconceivable to me that the rest of my family in Europe thought any different." He shrugged, then went on in a stronger voice as they continued down the aisle. "The British weren't letting any Jews into Palestine, of course, because `Great Britain's settled policy is not to upset the indigenous Arab population,' as the oh-so-proper young Foreign office man explained it to me down the length of his nose as he sat regally behind his desk in the British consulate in Brussels. But as we continued to chat, it turned out that Great Britain's `settled policy' was actually flexible enough to accommodate someone with a large knapsack full of untraceable uncut diamonds.

So I came to Netanya with my knapsack a little lighter, but not completely empty. There wasn't much here; the town was only ten years old and still made its living from growing oranges. But when the war came and the North African campaign really got rolling, the British turned the town into a convalescent center. It was truly horrible." Max Abramowitz got that faraway look again. "Sunlit, beautiful beaches, warm breezes, and instead of being covered with happy young people laughing, playing games, making love, all you had was a sea of wheelchairs filled with broken, bitter, suffering men, tended by nurses and doctors on the edge of exhaustion. We all did what we could, but what could a twenty-year old jeweler really do? I volunteered to help, I pushed the basket cases along the seaside, I talked and I listened. And as I talked and listened, I got an idea."

Max Abramowitz's expression shifted subtly, taking on a shrewd aspect David wasn't sure he liked. The old man's speech slowed a bit, and he began to enunciate his words with a cold precision very unlike the easy chattiness he had had before. This was business. "All those convalescent soldiers had three things in common: they were going home; they had girls in England they wanted to marry; and they had months of accumulated back pay. Now remember, David, this is back in 1942, and in 1942 diamonds were the exclusive province of the rich. It occurred to me that all these thousands of soldiers wanted to return from the wars bearing gifts for their sweethearts. What better gift than a diamond to symbolize their love, hmm? So I took my stock of great big rich man's diamonds, and I cut the stones into little quarter carat brilliants and set them into rings. And on my walks along the beach I talked and talked about something I called an `engagement ring.' It was fantastic!" Max Abramowitz's face shone with pride. "They couldn't buy them fast enough. And those little quarter carat stones were selling for ten times the price per carat of big stones. Everything was perfect, except for one small problem. I was running out of stones, and there was a war on. So how could I replenish my stock? Raw diamonds came from South Africa. Shipping them by sea was intolerably risky, the U-boats were still in control of the Atlantic. And jewelry was not exactly a high priority item for the limited air shipment capacity available. So it looked like I was stuck. But then I had another little idea.

"The big guns on the British tanks were taking a pounding from heavy use, and they were desperately trying to refinish the barrels. I pointed out to some of the people I had met that the fastest way to do this was to use diamond-tipped boring tools, and I volunteered to help them make them up right here. All I needed was to have some industrial diamonds shipped up from South Africa. And by the way, would it be possible to help me out by bringing along a commercial shipment for me at the same time? Of course it would be possible, we really appreciate your help, Mr. Abramowitz." The old man sighed with satisfaction. "I never had a supply problem throughout the war. And when it was over, I had a worldwide reputation on the buying and the selling end, and enough capital to take advantage of the middle-class diamond boom I had created. The question was: how?"

They had reached the other side of the enormous room. Two men were sitting on high stools behind a long table covered in black velvet on which was spread out the biggest array of unmounted diamonds David had ever seen. The men would reach out, pick up a stone from the table, examine it carefully with an eye loupe, weigh it on a precision balance, then make a few notations on the outside of an envelope and pop the stone inside before placing the envelope on a table behind them. Max Abramowitz reached out casually and picked up a stone. He held it up to the light and rotated it gently, watching the light sparkle. "The Midrash, the collection of the folk tales of the Jews, tells about a fabulous worm called the *shamir* used by King Solomon to build the temple in Jerusalem. The wonderful thing about the worm was that it could cut anything. The sages who wrote the story were talking about the diamond, David. Diamonds can cut through anything: glass, steel, granite. They could even cut through the Iron Curtain.

"The war was supposed to be over, but the Red Army was sitting on top of Eastern Europe, fomenting the revolutions that turned the Eastern Bloc into one big concentration camp. Well, they deserved it — they had been happy enough to shovel *us* into the ovens for Hitler. But the new Communist governments couldn't make anything work, the farm sector collapsed, and they had to import food. They couldn't pay their import bills with rubles or zlotys or any of their other worthless currencies, nobody would accept that *dreck*, that crap, so they were desperate for hard currencies.

"Well, what did they have to sell to raise the cash they needed? Something they didn't use themselves but that the decadent Westerners did? Diamonds, my boy, diamonds! The Russians were lousy with gem quality diamonds, their own and the ones they stole from their new satellites. There was just one little problem. Remember, this is the time of the Berlin airlift, the Americans weren't looking for peaceful coexistence, they didn't want to have anything to do with the Russians. But the Americans didn't mind dealing with me.

"Somehow, my name got mentioned in the right places, and in a little while I was buying uncut diamonds at *very* favorable prices from the East, cutting them, and selling them at *very* competitive prices in the West. Everybody was happy — the Russians got their cash, the Americans could continue boycotting their enemies and trading with their friends, and I was getting richer every day. The only people who were not so happy were the South Africans, because I was knocking the hell out of their monopoly pricing. On the other hand, I had grabbed such a big share of the total market that even de Beers couldn't refuse to sell through me. *A zoi geht es*, that's how it goes." Max Abramowitz tossed the diamond casually into the air, caught it deftly, and put it down gently on the velvet covered table. Then he took David's arm and escorted him back through the room, out through the security door, and down the yellow corridor past the managing director's office and out into the main lobby.

"So, David, what did you think?" The old man's face was beaming with pride. David thought he had every right to be proud, and said so. "It's an amazing story, Mr. Abramowitz. And actually sort of hopeful, if you know what I mean. After all, you're a Jew who's built a fortune by working peacefully with people who are our traditional enemies. It makes me feel as if there could be an end to all the hatred." Max Abramowitz's eyes darkened, and he seemed to fall into himself, to shrink a little. "I doubt it, David," he said ruefully. "There's always more than enough hate to go around."

CHAPTER 7

July 19, 1:00 P.M. EEST   **Naqoura, Lebanon**

D r. Fatimah Jemail removed the stethoscope from her ears, folded it slowly into an S-shaped mass and shoved it despondently into the pocket of her white hospital jacket. Then she reached forward and pulled the sheet roughly up over the child's face. The time for compassion was past.

She looked down the row of beds, each with its burden of misery, that filled the ward from wall to wall, and felt the bile of futility rising in her throat. No matter what she did in the ward, it would still be full tomorrow. The new ones would come, their faces shattered by shrapnel and flying concrete, their arms and legs broken, and for what? For following the will of Allah, sending rockets at the damned Jews, the damned infidel invaders. It was intolerable. But that was Arab life on the Israeli border in southern Lebanon. For now.

She walked down the aisle between two rows of beds, glancing at each chart as she passed. She paid no attention to the sullenly murderous faces behind the bandages. They would heal quickly, these young ones. Then they would return to the struggle. Until then, it didn't matter what they felt.

When she reached the main door of the UNIFIL field hospital in Naqoura, she stepped outside for a gasp of fresh air. The UN sentry stood at parade rest by the entrance, his Sten gun held easily by the flash suppressor, the butt resting against the highly polished combat boot half-hidden by the baggy leggings of his camouflage fatigues. His blond Norwegian face beneath the blue UN beret looked bored. Fatimah suppressed a shudder of distaste. More infidels, almost as bad as the Jews, these "peacekeepers." Precious little good they did.

Fatimah Jemail squinted against the glare and the dust. She was a large woman, wide in the hips, thick in the middle, lumpy at the top. She wore thick glasses with heavy frames, which made her naturally ugly face even uglier. Her bun of black hair formed an odd lump beneath the scrub cap she wore more out of modesty than for hygienic reasons. The overall effect was vaguely inhuman, and she knew it. But being both a woman and a physician was an anomaly in itself in her world, tolerated only by the UN, never accepted by her own people. But what could she do? She had taken her medical education in France so many years ago, when Lebanon was still a sinkhole of Western mimicry and corruption, before the defenders of the Faith had risen up to rekindle the lamp of piety and to expel the foreign influences. Now she was trapped by her profession, too westernized to turn her back on her education and take on a traditional woman's role, but newly guilty nonetheless. At least she could use her position to strike a blow for the restoration of her people's world.

And there, along the cobbled street that wound gently up the hill from the shuttle parking lot, was the girl, hurrying along, her feet raising little puffs of dust that merged and billowed out behind her like the train of a dress. Her nervous strides projected the trepidation that Hussein's story would undoubtedly have implanted in her. I wonder why Hussein enjoys that subtle kind of torture so much, Fatimah mused, why he is such a connoisseur of pain. Perhaps it is because he feels so much pain himself.

Fatimah waited silently, round face turned downward, pale, thin lips pressed unsmilingly together, until the girl panted all the way up the hill and stood sweating in front of her at the hospital entrance. Fatimah looked at the girl with grudging approval. At least the girl had had the good sense to wear a long black skirt and a long-sleeved dark blue blouse, not some obscene American outfit based on blue jeans. And the girl's Arabic was flawless.

"Dr. Jemail? I'm Jasmine Mahdin, I'm here to pick up the blood for Dr. Musawi, he called you, didn't he, I'm sure he did." It all came out in one breath, and then Jasmine stood there, winded, gently kicking one shoe against the other to rid them of some of their coat of dust. Fatimah couldn't help smiling. What a naive child, but a charming one nonetheless. "Yes, Miss Mahdin, he did indeed call. Please come inside." Fatimah Jemail turned in to the door. Jasmine Mahdin, manila envelope grasped firmly in her right fist, followed at her heels.

They turned left as Fatimah headed toward the blood bank, a prefabricated cold room that had been shoehorned into a corner. The insulated walls with their external network of coolant pipes jutted into the interior of the room. Fatimah looked at the mess with distaste. Always such crudity with the westerners, she thought, never any sense of beauty or balance or goodness, just the crass god of efficiency. She turned to check on Jasmine, and saw that the girl had fallen behind and was now staring horror-stricken across the ward, her left fist pressed against her lips. Fatimah walked back to her and placed a hand gently on her shoulder. Jasmine turned to her, her eyes wet. "All those children!" she half gasped, half whispered.

Fatimah tightened her grip on Jasmine's shoulder. "Yes," she said, "all those children. And there will be more tomorrow, and more the next day, and more the day after that. Until there is an end to the fighting, *inshallah*. So, please, Miss Mahdin, let us finish with your business so I can get back to helping them." She released Jasmine's shoulder, and the two of them continued on into the blood bank.

The sudden chill made Fatimah shiver, but it was a relief nonetheless. She walked down a narrow corridor between tiers of stainless steel shelving. On a shelf just above waist-level was an insulated plastic container with compartments for twelve pint bottles of blood. Fatimah pulled the container off the shelf by its padded handle, unlatched the top, checked the label on each bottle, and then latched the top closed again. She took the envelope from Jasmine, opened it and extracted a sheaf of forms. She reached into the pocket of her jacket, pulled out a worn ball-point pen, and had Jasmine sign each of the forms. Then she signed them herself, riffled through them expertly to select the ones she would need for her records, and put the remaining forms back in the envelope. She gave the envelope to Jasmine, then handed her the container of blood. Finally, as they headed back toward the blood bank door, Fatimah reached into a corner and extracted a wide mesh string bag stuffed with half a dozen plump yellow melons. She flashed Jasmine an ironic smile. "It's a bit macabre, I know, but refrigerated space is at a great premium here. And Hussein likes his melons just so." She handed Jasmine the string bag, then pushed by her to open the door.

As the two women walked out to the main entrance together, Fatimah was conscious of Jasmine repeatedly wrenching her gaze away from the bandaged heaps on the cots, only to find it wandering involuntarily back again. She is a soft one, Fatimah thought. She would not be very happy if she knew what was in those melons. But the messenger of life for our people is always a messenger of death for our enemies.

July 19, 7:00 P.M. IDT   **Netanya**

As Sid and he had agreed during a hurried breakfast, David arrived at the Netanya central bus station a few minutes before seven P.M. to meet Sid. As he wandered the colonnade lined with little shops, he was startled by a sudden commotion at one of the gates. A soldier had stopped a young woman waiting for the Jerusalem bus. As David walked closer, he thought the girl looked like Jasmine. Holy crap, he thought, it *is* Jasmine. He ran over to the gate just as Sid walked in. Sid saw David heading for trouble and immediately ran toward him.

Maybe it's not such a good idea to stick your nose into a situation you know nothing about, David thought. On the other hand, only a bum runs away from a friend in trouble. So David charged ahead, calling out "What are you doing in Netanya, Jasmine? And what the hell is going on?" Jasmine's jaw dropped when she saw David, but she recovered her poise quickly and replied that she had no idea what was going on, but this soldier seemed to think she was some kind of terrorist. The young soldier turned to David and suggested that he mind his own damn business – this was an Army matter. David didn't know what to do. Jasmine was no terrorist – but the soldier didn't know that, couldn't know that. As David turned back and forth from Jasmine to the soldier like a weathervane in a hurricane, Sid caught up with him and immediately took over. Flashing his military ID, he walked over to Jasmine and the soldier, who were now shouting at each other at the top of their respective lungs, and yelled "Cool it! Now, private, what is this all about?"

"Captain, I don't like the way she looks. She's carrying weird looking packages. So I started to grab them to do an inspection, at which point this hothead started bitching about her civil rights and wouldn't let go."

"Private, are you stationed here for security duty?"

"Well, no. But I thought…"

"Well you didn't think much! That uniform doesn't give you the right to shove people around just because you have a flash of paranoia." He turned to Jasmine. "The Army doesn't apologize, but I apologize anyway. This jerk had no right to mistreat you. Plus, David says you're OK."

As the chastened private slunk away, Jasmine rushed over to David, gave him a warm hug and rested her head on his shoulder. "My hero! Who is the heavyweight you brought in to save me?"

"Jasmine, meet my cousin, Captain Sid Goldman. I'm staying with Sid and his family for the vacation. But why are you here?"

Jasmine explained her situation, her father's emergency surgery, her sudden trip to Lebanon to bring back a supply of blood of an extremely rare type, and to bring back some fruit for one of the doctors who had performed her father's surgery. As she talked, she opened her packages to show that she was telling the truth. Even though she didn't need to.

My parents ship me fifty-six-hundred miles from home to keep me away from my girl, and she miraculously appears in front of me, thought David. I guess that's what they mean by *bashert*, destined.

The three of them took the bus back to Jerusalem. Jasmine headed straight to the hospital, and Sid and David headed back to Sid's house. Everything was fine.

Just fine.

July 19, 10:15 P.M. IDT   Jerusalem

Jasmine entered the lobby of the Hadassah Hospital, passed through the metal detector, waited for the security guard to check her packages, and walked up to the reception counter and asked to have Dr. Musawi paged. A few minutes later, Musawi appeared, all smiles and courtesy.

"Good evening, Miss Mahdin. How was the trip?"

"Depressing, Dr. Musawi. Have you been up to the UNIFIL hospital yourself? Have you seen the children's ward? It's horrible!"

She is soft, he thought. Too much time spent in America, land of sentimental cowards. "I've seen it, too" he said. "It's criminal. But it's the way non-Islamic countries always treat us, butchering our children. I suppose there is nothing to be done."

Jasmine bristled. "There is always something to be done! The Arab people don't have to tolerate brutality toward their children!"

Musawi felt unexpected elation, but didn't let it show on his face. *She can be recruited.* "We should talk about this some more," he said. "Perhaps tomorrow."

July 19, 10:30 P.M. EDT   *New York*

It was still hot in New York, and dark as Sam Hirsch drove across the 59th Street bridge and headed for the Long Island Expressway, affectionately known as the LIE, or less affectionately as the world's longest and narrowest parking lot. But not tonight. The white Mercedes S-550 sedan rolled silently through the night, unhindered by traffic. Sam liked his Mercedes. It was a Naziwagen, true, but it was named after a Jewish girl, Mercedes Jellinek. It cost too much money, but at least he had saved a little by refusing to get Barbara one too. She had to make do with a Lexus LX-570 SUV.

It had been a long day. He had parked the car at the garage at 51st Street and Eighth Avenue; stopped by the store to have a cup of coffee with his father; then spent the day taking cab ride after cab ride for a series of meetings with buyers for Bloomingdale's, Tiffany, and other stores whose jewelry departments sold trinkets to people with so little sense that they bought retail. But Sam was happy at the thought of getting home. He had the Bang and Olufsen Beosound system tuned to talk radio. It was entertaining to listen to the nut cases call in to rant.

The show host had the largest audience in the country. The evening's topic was threats to the U.S. by Middle Eastern fanatics. "Since 9/11, we know we need to take these threats seriously. But is taking off our shoes at the airport enough? Let's hear from our listeners. Hello, you're on the air."

Sam was not disappointed by the first caller. The radio emitted a semi-hysterical bleat. "Those camel-humping towelheads need a lesson!" Sam let out a guffaw. This guy was just too much. "The next time we hear them promise to destroy the Great Satan, we ought to nuke Mecca!" How original, thought Sam. I had hoped for something other than the same old clichés. He didn't have long to wait.

The next caller was way out of the ordinary; no shouting, no stuttering, no foaming at the mouth. Sam heard a calm, rather quiet voice with a faint Middle-Eastern accent saying "I can ignore your last caller's childish insults. What I cannot ignore is his blasphemous call to destroy the holiest city on Earth, the center of the One True Religion. We hear these crude threats even from some of your congressmen and senators. You must come to understand one great reality. All Muslims, all one billion of us, venerate Mecca. Any attack on Mecca is an attack on all of us and each one of us would indeed take it as a personal attack. We will someday have nuclear weapons, and we would use them, all of them, to destroy all of you. Muslims look forward to the day when Islam is triumphant worldwide, and we would welcome you into the universal society of Islam, *the Ummah*. But if you touch Mecca, we will accept your total extermination as the second best outcome. I do not say this as a threat, but as a prediction." There was a definitive click as the caller hung up.

Sam reached forward and turned the radio off. That didn't sound like your average call-in, he thought. This sounds like something to be taken seriously.

July 20, 12:00 noon IDT   Jerusalem

Jasmine Mahdin sat in a secluded corner of the Hadassah Hospital cafeteria. Across from her at the small table was Dr. Hussein Musawi, sipping his sweet mint tea. He put down his cup and said "I'm glad that you wanted to talk with me about what the skirmishes on the Israel-Lebanon border are doing to Lebanese children." said Musawi, "I understand how wrenching the experience of seeing the mutilated children in Lebanon must have been. I too have seen their suffering. And I am sure you would like to help stop it."

"Of course I would like to help. But what could I do? Protest? Carry signs? Throw rocks?" She sighed. "That kind of thing takes years to have any effect."

Musawi was pleased. Her response was not the kind of idiocy he expected from an American college student, full of self-righteousness and the belief that media-oriented posturing would change the world. It was time to open the window a bit. "That is exactly the point," he said, leaning forward across the table to emphasize his words. He looked directly into her eyes and continued "Most groups that resist the Israeli occupation are content to throw rocks at soldiers, to shoot at passing cars, to fire pathetic rockets that hit nothing. But there are a few of us who believe that it will take something more, much more, to change the status quo."

Jasmine was taken aback. She had expected this conversation to evolve into a discussion of ways she could help with a relief effort, not a discussion of geopolitical cataclysm. But the Arab cultural habit of deference to men automatically led her to maintain a calm exterior. "I wonder if there is a chance that the new agreement between the Israeli government and the Arab League will lead to rapid improvements. Perhaps that's a more certain way to get help to the children."

Musawi tried to suppress his inner fury at the thought of that cursed agreement, that testament to the cowardice of the corrupt princelings who dominated the councils of the Arab League. This girl would react badly to an emotional explosion. But he could not return to perfect calm. His voice hardened. "I wish that were so. But the Israelis are not to be trusted. They will talk, they will drag their heels, and nothing will actually happen. We will need another fact on the ground, and we will need one soon. When that comes about, we will need spokespeople in America to explain why what has happened, has happened. I hope you will be one of them. But now I must get back to work. Have a good rest of the day." He rose and left the room.

Jasmine did not get up, but sat marshaling her thoughts. What is he talking about? Facts on the ground? Dr. Musawi doesn't talk like any doctor I've ever met before, she thought. He sounds like a politician. Or something.

CHAPTER 8

Early morning, and Sergeant Shmuel Gradsteyn was making the 35 mile drive in to work at Launch Complex 4, head pounding, eyes bleary and bloodshot, breath foul. Like always. "I was an engineer in Moscow, but now I'm just a fucking mechanic here in the Holy Land. Holy, my ass." His thoughts rolled past like mental billboards. Like always. What a shitty job.

But at least that damned Arab Musawi was making it a little more worthwhile. What the hell should he care if the little fucker wanted to steal some technology? Copies of a few manuals, photos of a few control panels, a spare circuit board nobody would ever miss. He'd get enough money out of this little transaction to move into a better apartment, buy a better car, buy better vodka, maybe even get a girlfriend who would be worth something in the sack, in contrast to that revolting blob of a wife he was cursed with.

He went through the security ritual at the gate, parked the car, and headed down into the bowels of Launch Complex 4. He looked at the maintenance schedule and set to work. Four hours later, he had his opportunity. "Keep an eye on things, Sergeant," said Captain

Yehudah Levin. "We need to get out of this dungeon for a couple of minutes." Gradsteyn grunted a sour assent. Act normal, he thought, even though those idiots were handing him a small fortune. Then Levin and Eytalon headed up the staircase to join the rest of the staff for a bite of lunch out in the open air. It wasn't strictly allowed by regulations for both officers to leave the launch panel at the same time, but what harm could it do?

Gradsteyn went to work with unprecedented speed and concentration. Forget about the headache, the nausea, the whole hangover. Money motivates men, they say. Damn right. He pulled out his cellphone and began feverishly snapping pictures of the control panels with the phone's eight megapixel camera. He next flipped through the operating manuals, photographing each page. Then he ran over to the storage room, quickly grabbed the spare circuit board the Arab had asked for, and shoved it into his lunch pail. Everything was back to normal when Levin and Eytalon scrambled back down the steps, wiping crumbs from their mouths.

Five more hours and his shift was over. He lumbered up the staircase, plopped into his car, and headed home. Just another day at the office.

July 21, 5:30 P.M. IDT   Jerusalem

Hussein Musawi sat in a corner of the pizza shop on Hamaayan Street, pleased by the impenetrable chaos produced by the evening crowd. After all, that was why he had chosen this spot for the meeting. He sipped his mint tea, and waited.

Shmuel Gradsteyn lumbered in, eyes bloodshot, civilian clothes unkempt, carrying a small red vinyl briefcase. It had a cheap brass clasp on the flap with a little sliding button to release it. He sat down next to Musawi. Musawi sipped more tea to suppress the nausea induced by the smell of vodka and an unbathed body. But the animal appeared to have done his work.

Gradsteyn pushed the briefcase along the floor so it rested at Musawi's feet. "There it is – everything! Now, I want my money." Musawi smiled softly. "And you shall have it." Musawi pushed a briefcase identical to the one he had received across the floor to Gradsteyn. "This briefcase contains 250 thousand shekels. If you have any sense, you will not put it in the bank. You will also not spend too much of it too fast. That way, no one will know about our little transaction." Until it's far too late, Musawi thought.

Without a word, Gradsteyn picked up the briefcase and walked out of the shop. He didn't notice the Arab kid walk out after him and take up a position ten steps behind. He came to the curb and stopped to wait for a break in the traffic. The kid elbowed his way through the crowd (in Israel, nobody notices it when you shove them – shoving is standard procedure) to stand directly behind Gradsteyn. As Gradsteyn stepped off the curb, the kid quietly reached forward, grasped the brief-case handle, gently slipped a hypodermic needle into Gradsteyn's back, emptied the contents into his heart, and quickly pulled the needle out and shoved it into his pocket. Gradsteyn collapsed in a heap, the apparent victim of a heart attack. The kid walked calmly away. It wasn't a good idea to waste money. It also wasn't a good idea to leave loose ends.

July 21, 10:30 P.M. IDT   ***Jerusalem***

David, Sid, and the family were sitting at the table, relaxing after a late dinner of yogurt, tabouli, fruit, and coffee, when the call came through, on the land line, not on the cell phone. Unusual. Sid's wife Nina answered, then turned to Sid with the resigned sigh of military wives everywhere. "Sid, it's for you." Who else? Sid rose and took the handset from his wife. "Shalom! This is Sid Goldman."

"Sid, this is Dov Kafni." Trouble already. Kafni was military police. Sid had met him a few times, and Kafni had impressed him as unflappable. He wasn't the kind of guy to call you at home on a whim. "Something peculiar has happened," Kafni continued. "One of your mechanics just turned up dead. Shmuel Gradsteyn."

Sid broke in "I don't find that so peculiar. The guy drank a bottle of vodka every night, like the rest of the Russians. The only thing with more alcohol in it was a lizard in a specimen bottle at the museum. The reason he wasn't booted out on his ass was that he was a great mechanic, plus we felt we had an obligation to take care of an immigrant. I'm surprised he didn't drop dead before this."

Kavni was annoyed at the interruption. "Let me finish. That's what I thought, too, at first. He had a stroke or a heart attack. But since he dropped dead on the street, we did an autopsy. His family didn't object. None of those Russians are religious, so they didn't care. And I don't think they liked him much anyway. But here's the point. When they got him up on the table, they found a puncture wound on his back that looked like it had been made with a hypodermic needle, and they found a corresponding puncture wound in his heart. So they ran some specimens through toxicology, and it turns out that he had been poisoned. A shot of potassium chloride right into the heart muscle. Somebody murdered him. Now, people get killed all the time. Maybe he owed somebody money. Maybe he played around with the wrong guy's wife. But when somebody who works in the missile command is killed, it rings the alarm bells. I think you'd better ratchet up your security."

Sid hung up the phone slowly, and sat down, staring off into space. "Sid, what's' happening?" Nina asked. "I don't' know," Sid answered slowly, "but we may have a problem."

July 22, 7:12 A.M . AST Abqaiq City, Saudi Arabia
The Boeing 707 heavy transport with Pakistani air force markings on the tail, a square green flag outlined in yellow gold with the crescent and star, circled the Abqaiq Airport. It was unusual for a military plane to land at Abqaiq, since it was a little used civilian airfield once owned by Aramco, but this plane did not intend to spend any time under observation by the U.S. military personnel stationed at the Prince Sultan Airbase near Riyadh. The special freight handling crew, all members of ISI, the Pakistani Inter-Services Intelligence agency, rechecked the cargo restraints for the hundredth time. This was one cargo that should not, could not, be permitted to shift on touchdown.

Landing clearance obtained, the 707 banked for final approach and landed smoothly. It then parked on an obscure taxiway at the end of the main runway, engines still running. The cargo bay doors opened, and there was a whine as the cargo elevator descended, carrying a large crate secured to a wheeled cart. The ISI crew coupled the cart to a small tractor, usually used to transport aircraft from a hanger to an active gate. The tractor pulled the cart over to the rear of an ordinary looking white unmarked tractor-trailer. The oversized diesel engine under the hood and the super-duty shock absorbers and leaf springs were unobservable.

The ISI crew unhooked the restraining straps, and gently rolled the cart onto the trailer lift gate. The lift gate rose, and the non-uniformed Saudi army personnel in the trailer rolled the cart into the truck and slammed the trailer door shut. Without a word, the ISI men turned and returned to the 707. The pilot turned the plane around, taxied back to the runway, and took off heading east. The driver of the truck started the engine, drove the rig through a gate in the airport fence, and headed down a service road into the desert.

Two hours later, the truck pulled into a patch of sand surrounded by a twelve foot high chain link fence topped with barbed wire. The only structure inside the fence was a sheet metal building about forty feet on a side. The truck drove through the open door of the building. The truck doors were thrown back, and the army personnel pushed the cart onto the lift gate and lowered it to the floor. White coated men swarmed over the crate on the cart and quickly pried it open. The crate contained a heavy cylindrical metal can with a digital control panel embedded in one side.

   Saudi Arabia now possessed a nuclear bomb. Within
two weeks, they would have nineteen more.

July 22, 10:30 A.M . IDT   Jerusalem

Professor Nihad Zaki of the Department of Aerospace
Engineering at the Israel Institute of Technology, familiarly known as the Technion, had just finished his morning lecture on inertial navigation instrumentation to the
graduate students enrolled in Aerospace Engineering
Course 086759 "Navigation and Guidance Systems."
He walked back to his office, sat down at his desk, and
poured himself a cup of coffee from the stainless steel
thermos he kept for his exclusive use. His colleagues
thought it was a little strange that he didn't just stop by
the cafeteria like everyone else, but had finally decided
that he had some phobia about germs. He never disillu-
sioned them. But he really kept his coffee private because
he didn't want it touched by the goddamned Jews.

   Zaki was the only Arab on the Aerospace Engineering
faculty. None of his colleagues seemed to care about that;
scientists are a cosmopolitan lot. What they couldn't
know was that he was a Hamas agent.

   Zaki had just raised the cup to his lips when the
office door opened and he saw Hussein Musawi standing in the doorway, carrying a brown paper bag. Musawi
walked in, closed the door, pulled down the shade on the
glass panel in the door, and sat down on the chair ordinarily used by students coming in to discuss problems.
Without any preamble, Musawi got to the point. He
handed Zaki the brown paper bag. "We have obtained
a guidance board from a Sabra missile. You don't need
to know how. You are to reprogram the targeting chip

for the coordinates of Tel Aviv. We need it within two weeks. Will you have any problem doing that?"

Zaki was thunderstruck. He had never hoped for such a triumph! Controlling his jubilation, he said "Of course there is no problem! I will get it done immediately. And I hope you make good use of it." "Oh I will," said Hussein Musawi, smiling. "I will."

July 22, 1:30 P.M. IDT   Netanya

Herman Schneiderman hated being away from his Manhattan apartment. The East 80's were very pleasant. Also posh. He had a Marazzi Designs kitchen that had cost him three hundred thousand bucks, and a gorgeous Brazilian cook who knew how to use it, as well as to do some other equally pleasant things. He had a Limestone Gallery bathroom with a carwash shower and a seventy five thousand dollar Isis toilet hand-set with Swarovski crystals. It made him feel like he was pooping on diamonds. He had a living room, furnished by Baker, that had an enormous curved window with a panoramic view over the East River. Why should he ever leave it?

He also hated flying. He hated takeoffs. He hated cruising at altitude. He hated landings. He also hated heat. He also hated falafel. So why was he sitting on a bench by the beach in Netanya, five thousand six hundred and thirteen miles from Manhattan, sweating in the sun and eating a pita bread rolled around falafel and salad? Because sometimes you had to do hateful things to make money, a lot of money. And Israel was a good place to make a lot of money if you knew what you were doing. Herman always knew what he was doing. He was an industrial spy.

Israel may be a tiny country, but it is a technology giant, especially in military technology. Half the countries in the world, even those who claim they hate Israel, rely on Israeli companies to invent and produce the communications networks, drones, airborne electronics, antiaircraft missiles, and other assorted goodies that enable them to continue to beat each other's brains out, year after year. Where there's that much good stuff, there is more than enough to steal. When Willie Sutton, the great bank robber, was asked why he robbed banks, his answer was "Because that's where the money is." Same principle.

Herman sat on the bench, his chubby bespectacled face showing its usual calm. He was waiting to meet his contact. A couple of afternoons surfing the Web, a little judicious hacking of Facebook, and he had a good idea of who might have access to Israeli Military Technologies, Inc.'s high speed communications hardware. IMT itself wasn't a good place to look. They paid their people very generously, and were very supportive of staff members who wanted to go off on their own. Stay friendly, and you can work out profitable cross-licensing agreements if the spin-off clicks. If not, well, you can always hire your friends back. But IMT's customers were another matter. And IMT's big customer was the IDF, the Israeli Defense Forces. The army.

Everybody is on Facebook. Even the president of China. Even Israeli army officers. Even Israeli army officers with lousy credit reports and outstanding judgments. So Herman had sent out a broadcast "Friend me" request to the officers who looked like viable prospects, and "Bingo!" he had hooked Major Ari Romach. And after a few exchanges, he had arranged to meet in person because he was going to be in Israel on business. Monkey business, but Ari didn't need to know that until after they met.

He didn't have to wait long. Major Romach, not even sweating in the heat, walked up to him and said "Herman?" Ari looked encouragingly dishonest. He glanced over his shoulder every few seconds. Herman rose to shake hands. "It's good to meet you in the flesh, Ari. Computer screens have their limitations." Both men sat down and gazed out at the Mediterranean. Herman continued, "I think we can do each other some good. You know, I mentioned that I'm in the technology brokerage business. I connect up companies that can use each other's patented products to enhance their own products. I have a client that thinks they are a fit with IMT's communications servers. I got in touch directly with IMT, but they are awfully close-mouthed about their capabilities. All I've been able to get out of them is marketing hype. I need more." Ari saw what was coming, but played a little slow. "You know I don't work for IMT." "I know," said Herman, "but you do use their communications equipment. In fact, you said that you maintain an installation that uses it. So you know exactly how well it performs. And you have access to all the operating manuals and schematic diagrams. My client could really use copies of those. They would be grateful for those copies. Very grateful. In fact, very, very grateful."

Herman watched closely as Ari made his internal calculations. How much would it take to pay off his credit card debt? Pay his back rent? Pay his gambling debts? Ari replied slowly. "I might be able to help you. I would have difficulties if anyone found out I had given you those copies. But for 150,000 shekels, I could take the risk." Herman relaxed. 150,000 shekels, about $75,000, was chump change, cigarette money. He was in. "I'm sure my client would find that acceptable. Why don't we meet next week and exchange gifts? Same day, same time." Ari nodded and walked off.

Ari was pleased. The little weasel had fallen into the trap that Ari had carefully built over the past six months, creating an identity that would pull in the sleaziest players. Mossad was extremely good at providing disinformation. Herman had just earned himself a place on the soon-to-be-indicted-slime-ball list.

July 26, 9:15 A.M . IDT   Jerusalem

The conference room was mildly depressing, grey walls, metal chairs, a formica conference table. But Dov Kafni didn't notice. He had had so many meetings in the room, it felt like home. Today the meeting was his weekly sit-down with Ari Romach of Mossad, just to compare notes. The military police and Mossad always stayed in close touch.

Sipping from the Styrofoam cup of bad coffee, Ari opened the conversation. "I've had an interesting contact this week. As you know, for the last six months, I've built up a false identity as a corruptible officer. We have a major operation going, trolling for information traffickers. This week I struck gold. I had a meet with a major industrial spy from America, Herman Schneiderman, who is trying to get his hands on operational data for our telecommunications equipment used for command and control. He says he's going to sell it to some U.S. electronics firm."

Dov leaned back reflectively, the front legs of his chair lifting slightly from the floor. "I've heard about this Schneiderman guy. He was mixed up in some plutonium deal in the Ukraine, as I remember." "Yes he was," Ari replied, "but not in a way anyone could prove. The only person who had indicated he was willing to talk about Schneiderman's role died suddenly of an apparent heart attack before he could provide any really useful information." Dov sat up abruptly, the front legs of his chair smacking the floor with a loud crack. "That's genuinely disturbing, Ari, because we've just had one of our missile techs drop dead of an apparent heart attack. Only the heart attack wasn't a heart attack. The guy was murdered, pretty cleverly, too. And it happened just when Schneiderman was in town. I think we should put a tight tail on him."

July 27, 10:20 A.M . IDT   **Jerusalem**

The beginning of Ramadan was less than two weeks away. Colonel Zvi ben-Aryeh sat at his desk, making up the duty rosters for the next month. On the first day of Ramadan, the operations staff would be his special group: Avram Gush (the propulsion engineer) was slotted in as the first launch officer; Shimon Naphtali (the guidance system technician) was slotted in as the communications officer; and Jonah Frischman (the warhead specialist), and Menachem Aronot (the silo mechanic) would fulfill their accustomed roles. He thought of them as The Usual Suspects. Gallows humor.

They had met ten times over the last several weeks, working out the plan in exquisite detail. It all boiled down to defeating the safety procedures developed to stop crazy men from setting off a nuclear war. The procedures were not designed, however, for his kind of crazy men. Crazy men who were inside the system, who knew every detail of how the whole nuclear missile system worked.

The mechanics of activating the missile were straightforward. The procedure for getting it done without alerting anyone was not. Every missile silo in the world is under constant surveillance by satellites run by the intelligence services of every technologically advanced nation. Any visible launch preparations would be known to the world within minutes of their initiation.

Further, the Israeli army kept a tight rein on its nuclear missiles. Sensors were installed at every access point to the missile and its interior, sensors that would transmit an instant warning to military bases around the country, and to rapid reaction squads that would be helicoptered to the site as quickly as possible.

Despite all these precautions, the missile could be hijacked. It would take under an hour to arm the bomb and launch the missile on its one-way trip to Mecca without alerting a soul.

First, Menachem would break the seals on the main control panel, bypass the intrusion alarm on the silo access doors and on the hemispherical weather doors at the top of the tube, and release the access door locks. Then he would open the access door, enter the silo, climb the internal ladder to the weather doors, and break the physical door seals. Then he would wait.

Jonah and Avram would follow Menachem into the silo. Jonah would run up the ladder. He would bypass the alarm on the missile hatch protecting the nuclear bomb, open it, and disconnect the arming circuit that required an arming code which was supposed to be sent from Jerusalem over an encrypted hard-wired link. He would then connect his own arming device, arm the bomb, scramble down the ladder and reenter the control room.

Avram would climb down the ladder to the exhaust nozzles. He would remove the safety interlocks on the solid fuel igniters, and rig a direct electrical connection bypassing the secure ignition sequencer. Then he would head back to the control room.

During this process, Shimon would open the back of the master guidance computer which programs the onboard controller that manages the nozzle and tailfin servos which guide the missile in flight. The computer is connected to the missile by an electrical umbilical which disconnects at launch. He would pull the inte-grated circuit chip containing the control information for the location of the default target for the missile, and substitute the Mecca chip prepared by ben-Aryeh.

None of these preparations would be visible from outside the silo, and none of the alarms would have been triggered. It would now be time to dispense with secrecy. Ben-Aryeh would signal Menachem, and Menachem would energize the weather door motor and return to the control room. The hemispherical doors would yawn open. Every spy satellite would detect the opening, but it would be too late to do anything about it. Ben-Aryeh would push the red button, fire would explode from the silo, and the missile would surge forth on its mission of vengeance.

CHAPTER 9

Beneath the street in the Old City, the Hamas cell pored intently over the documents and circuit boards procured for them by the late but unlamented Shmuel Gradsteyn. The Israelis were too diligent for their own good. The procedures for maintaining and launching the missiles were excruciatingly clear and detailed. They could override the safety interlocks in less than fifteen minutes. Professor Zaki had reprogrammed the stolen guidance board with the coordinates of their target. It was not as perfect as the original targeting program it replaced, which was designed to achieve pinpoint accuracy for targets many hundreds of miles away, but it didn't need to be. It was only 20 miles from Netanya to Tel Aviv.

Tel Aviv.

Erase Tel Aviv, the financial and cultural center of modern Israel, and the life would go out of the occupier state. Half a million of the sons of pigs and monkeys would vanish in a flash of flame. So would their banks and investment banking houses, their theaters, their museums. So would their courage. And then… Then the country would see a mass exodus, a reverse *aliyah*, as thousands of people ran for the exits, heading to America to beg sanctuary from their soft, fat relatives. The army would fall apart as recriminations echoed down the halls. The government would collapse. And then the hated Jews would be easy prey for the advancing tide of Islamic armies that would descend on them. They would be driven into the sea. Not one would survive. It would mean total victory.

Musawi felt a spiritual elation envelop him. The pieces were now all in place. Victory would be theirs on the first day of Ramadan.

Ramadan Mubarak! Blessed Ramadan!

August 3, 9:20 A.M . IDT   Jerusalem

Sid Goldman was still uneasy. That Gradsteyn business kept gnawing at him. He sat at his cluttered desk at missile command, deep in thought. A coffee cup sat next to him on his desk, its contents cold and untasted. Who would assassinate that *schicker*, that drunk? And for what? Gradsteyn certainly had had a security clearance, he needed one to work on missiles at all, but he was just a mechanic. He didn't know anything that important. Did he?

Why and who, those are the issues, he thought. Unconsciously, his mind slipped back into the rhythms of Talmudic disputation he had learned as a kid in New York. He would sit with his great uncle, David's *zayde*, at the kitchen table, a volume of Talmud open in front of them. The Talmud was the intellectual fountainhead of Judaism, containing commentary by the rabbis on the bible and on the laws and traditions that had come down by word of mouth until they were finally reduced to writing around 200 A.D. The pages were oddly organized, the basic discussion in the middle of the page, then discussions of the discussion by later rabbis surrounding the basic discussion. And sometimes discussions of the discussions of the discussions around those. Raise a question, try an answer, rebut the answer, which raises another question, which requires another answer, and so on until finally you reached a satisfying conclusion. Or not. But usually it worked. So here we go. Let's start with why.

Surreptitiously squirting a syringe full of potassium chloride into somebody's heart is not exactly a standard murder method. It's a lot easier to shoot somebody, or stab them, or hit them over the head. And you don't do it on a crowded street in broad daylight, either. You use a dark alley, or a doorway, or a staircase landing. So why this method?

Because you don't want anyone to realize they're dealing with a murder, that's why. A man drops dead reasonably quietly on a public street, it's a heart attack, of course. Jews eat too much salt and cholesterol. But why don't you want anybody to realize it's a murder?

Always follow the money. Are you the beneficiary of a life insurance policy on him? Gradsteyn hadn't been a rich man, but he certainly had his army insurance at least. He also wasn't a nice man, so his wife might have wanted the money more than she wanted him. Sid started to make a to-do list. First, check out whether Gradsteyn had any insurance. Have a chat with his widow. But this didn't seem likely. Gradsteyn's wife was unlikely to have been a clandestine hit-wife, and it's hard to imagine her knowing enough to hire an assassin with the skills to pull this job off.

Do you want to shut him up? That sounds a little better, dead men tell no tales, unless they end up in the forensic pathology lab, and who would expect that to happen? So somebody didn't want Gradsteyn to spill the beans. What beans?

What beans, what beans, what beans?

Sid sat back in his chair to clear his head. He took a sip of the ice cold coffee, felt like spitting it out, but drank the rest of it anyway. Then he got up from his desk, walked across the room to the coffee station near the door, poured another cup, walked back to his desk and started thinking again.

Maybe I should stop thinking about why, and start thinking about who, Sid thought. Who knows that potassium chloride is both lethal and almost undetectable? People who read too many medical novels and spy thrillers. And doctors. And spies.

Why would a spy want to bump Gradsteyn off? (Bump him off, oh boy, the New York kid in me is waking up again.) But even if Gradsteyn didn't know much, he had access to a great deal of secret material, like operating manuals and missile spare parts. So let's think about the spy angle. Suppose Gradsteyn got turned. Suppose he pilfered technical information and provided it to someone. The value of the information drops like a stone if anybody knows it's missing, since counter-measures will be put in place immediately. So someone wants him silenced. Permanently. Sid added a second item to his list. Check the inventory at the silo where Gradsteyn worked.

August 4, 7:50 A.M.   ***Near Netanya***

Sid Goldman hopped out of his jeep as it drew up to the missile silo entrance at Launch Complex 4. Yehuda Levin was waiting at the door. "What's up? You didn't give us much notice that you were coming out." Sid shrugged. "Something unexpected popped up." He didn't want to reveal any details to anyone on the site, not at this point. "We just need to do a quick manual and spares check." Sid and Levin proceeded down the stairs into the control room.

Sid first examined the manual library, which filled a steel bookcase fixed to the wall next to the control console. He checked off the titles on the shelf against a copy of the manual inventory list. Nothing was missing, but something seemed faintly wrong. The manuals were slightly out of order. Several of the guidance system loose leaf binders had been shelved next to the propulsion system interlock binders. Why would somebody be that careless? Had somebody been in a rush to get them back on the shelves?

He next entered the spares locker, and began methodically checking the shelves against the master inventory list. Bin after bin checked out correctly, until he came to the bin containing spare guidance system circuit boards. He was one short. He left the spares locker and walked over to the bookcase, pulled out the maintenance log, and scanned the entries dated after the last inventory check. None of the guidance system circuit boards had been replaced since the prior inventory. So a board really was missing.

Not good.

Sid gave a cursory goodbye to Levin and the other members of the crew, headed up the steps, climbed into the jeep, and drove off toward Netanya. Several miles down the road, when he was out of sight of the launch complex, he pulled over to the side of the road. He removed his secure cellphone from a concealed compartment under the dashboard, and dialed the special number linking him to Dov Kafni. "We have an issue, Dov. There has been some kind of security breach at Gradsteyn's silo. It's time to pull in Schneiderman."

August 5, 12:50 P.M. IDT   Netanya

It was a beautiful day, and David and Jasmine had taken the bus up to Netanya for some relaxation. David had insisted. He could see that Jasmine was exhausted from the strain of endlessly sitting in the hospital. She hadn't wanted to go at first, but her father was recuperating satisfactorily, and David convinced her that it was safe to take a day away.

They walked south along the promenade overlooking the Netanya beach, luxury hotels to their left, a steep drop to the beach on their right. The azure Mediterranean sparkled in the sunlight, a living travel brochure cliché, but spectacular nonetheless. It formed an unlikely background for a conversation more suited to a windowless room with deadbolt locks on the door.

Jasmine seemed lost in thought. "Come on, Jasmine, lighten up. Things are going very well for your father. It's OK for you to be happy. At least a little happy."

Jasmine shook her head. "I'm not worrying about my father. It's something else that keeps troubling me. David, I had a very strange conversation with one of my father's surgeons a few weeks ago. I had told him how upset I was at seeing the children who had been injured in the fighting at the border in Lebanon. He said that he would like to talk about it further, and we had lunch together in the cafeteria at the hospital. I assumed that he wanted to talk about opportunities to help with some relief project, raising money for medical supplies and staff. But it was nothing like that. He just talked in vague political terms about the need to change the situation by some spectacular act. He talked about a new fact on the ground. I don't know whether to be worried or not."

David wasn't very concerned. "Look, Jasmine, nobody likes the current situation. How many wild men did we hear on the Columbia campus every day, proclaiming a revolution for one reason or another? And none of them was about to actually do anything. Talk is cheap. Your doctor was just venting."

Jasmine shook her head doubtfully. "You're probably right. But I can't get over the feeling that there's something more to it." David put his arm around her shoulders and gave a little squeeze. "Well, I can't blame you for that. Let's see if he raises the subject again. If he does, that will be time enough to worry. In the meantime, let's just enjoy our walk, get some dinner, and take the bus back to Jerusalem. We'll leave the worrying to Shin Bet. Right now, it's somebody else's problem." To himself he said "I hope."

August 5, 1:30 P.M. IDT Jerusalem

The interrogation room looked just like the ones on television crime shows like NCIS. No windows, an eight foot long grey metal table with four chairs along one side and a single chair on the other side facing a large panel of one-way glass. Microphones were on the table, and a video camera recorded everything going on in the room. The walls were painted grey too, and the room was illuminated by a simple two bulb fluorescent fixture. Schneiderman sat calmly in the single chair, alone in the room. He wasn't worried. In his line of country, sitting in an interrogation room was business as usual. He had done it many times, and had never failed to walk out again unscathed, and in particular, unindicted. He knew where too many bodies were buried for anyone to want to put him on public trial.

The door opened. Sid Goldman and Dov Kavni walked into the room and sat down directly opposite Schneiderman. Kavni was carrying a maroon accordion folder latched closed with a string. He unwound the string, opened the folder, pulled out a stack of papers, and slammed them down hard on the table. "What kind of schmuck does he think I am," thought Schneiderman, "trying such a worn-out psychological stunt? The noise is supposed to frighten me? Fella, you're an amateur. You should be looking for another line of work."

Kavni didn't waste any time. "We know what you do for a living. Ordinarily, we'd just set up a sting, wait for you to bite, and put you away for a couple of years. In fact, we were right in the middle of doing just that. You know your friend Ari Romach, the crooked officer who was going to get you all that communications information? He's Mossad, Schneiderman. But we terminated the operation before you paid him off, because we think you were talking to somebody else as well. And that somebody is now dead of unnatural causes. So you're not just looking at an industrial espionage charge. You're looking at first degree murder."

Schneiderman swallowed hard. "Murder? I'm just a technology buyer! Maybe I use methods that are a little unorthodox, but I'm not a violent man. And I wasn't talking to anybody except Ari."

Kavni pulled a photograph of Gradsteyn from the pile of documents, an eight by ten blowup of the one from his security pass, and slapped it down on the table in front of Schneiderman. "Recognize this guy?" he asked. Schneiderman looked closely at the photo. "No. Who is he?" Kavni snorted in disgusted disbelief. "*Was*, Schneiderman, not *is*. His name was Shmuel Gradsteyn. He was a tech in the missile command, with access to the same kind of documents you were trying to bribe Ari to obtain. And just when you turn up in Israel, he turns up dead. So we think you know something about what happened. And, believe me, you are going to tell us."

Schneiderman was sweating. "There's nothing to tell. Even if you pull out my fingernails, there's nothing for me to say." Mentally kicking himself, he thought "I shouldn't have given them the idea." But, he also thought, Israel is a civilized country right? They don't do that kind of thing here. Do they?

Kavni rocked back in his chair, lifting the front legs off the floor, and stared at the ceiling. "All right, Schneiderman, we'll play it your way. You are now under indefinite detention. Let us know when you're ready to talk." He rocked his chair forward onto all four legs, got up and knocked on the door. It opened to reveal two army officers, who entered and escorted Schneiderman, still protesting, out into the corridor.

Sid turned to Kavni. "What do you think? He was scared, sure, but he also looked genuinely surprised. That's hard to fake." Kavni was considerably more cynical. "Not that hard for him. He makes his living by lying, and he makes a very good living. Let's see how he feels after another couple of days in a cell, a very uncomfortable cell. We've got plenty of time to sort this out."

Plenty of time.

Sid left the meeting unsatisfied. Maybe Kavni had more experience, but Sid was sure that Schneiderman wasn't lying. He walked down the featureless corridor, hands in his pockets, thinking furiously. He walked out of the security building and sat down on a bench. Again, using his Talmudic method of thinking, he started a chain of argument. So, assume Schneiderman wasn't lying. Who else would want operational information on an Israeli nuclear missile silo, and want it enough to kill for it? The countries with intelligence services competent to pull off this kind of operation, America, Russia, Pakistan, China, already had missiles and nuclear weapons. It wasn't a government operation.

If it wasn't a government entity, then what kind of group was it? And whoever they were, what were they going to do with the information? They were either going to use it themselves, or sell it to someone who would use it. How would they use it? They would use it to launch the missile.

Sid didn't like the place his thoughts were taking him, but he kept going. Now, who would want to steal information that would allow them to launch a missile? That would depend on their target. If the target was outside Israel, it would be fanatic Jewish settlers from the West Bank. If the target was inside Israel, it would be Islamic terrorists. One way or another, thought Sid, I think that some homicidal nutcases are trying to get their fingers on the nuclear trigger, and they have every intention of pulling it.

August 7, 7:25 A.M . IDT   Jerusalem

Colonel Zvi ben-Aryeh looked haggard. Waiting for action was wearing him down. He wasn't sleeping much, and he was drinking six cups of coffee a day to stay sharp. Or at least awake. He wasn't worried about the plan; it was perfect. But the longer they had to wait, the more chances there were for things to go wrong. He could get run over by a bus, which wasn't that improbable, considering how Israelis drive. One of his team could also get run over by a bus. Or get food poisoning. Or have a stroke. Hell, one of my mechanics, that drunken Russian, just dropped dead of a heart attack. He shook his head to clear it. Cut it out, he thought, this worrying is insane. Just do your job. You're a soldier, right? Well, an awful lot of soldiering is waiting. And this is worth waiting for, really worth waiting for.

Sid Goldman glanced across the room at ben-Aryeh. Boy, he looks like hell, Sid thought. Something is definitely going on. The Colonel always has a razor-sharp crease in his pants and a spit shine on his boots. Today he looks like he slept on a grate. Sid turned back to his computer monitor and pulled up the duty rosters for the next five days. A big part of his supervisory responsibility was to keep tabs on the operational personnel. You never knew when the Arabs were going to try another sneak attack like the Yom Kippur War of 1973, and you had to mobilize in what his college friends from Texas called a "New York minute." You needed to know who was where all the time.

Now that was odd. The schedule for most of the month was perfectly ordinary, but the schedule for August 8 decidedly was not. Usually each silo was staffed by personnel who often worked together, who were chosen to be of similar age and background to minimize the possibility of conflict among men with their fingers on the nuclear button. There were no fixed teams, but there wasn't that much variation, either. The crew for Launch Complex 4 for August 8 looked like The Odd Couple, or The Odd Quartet, actually. As far as he could remember, and Sid prided himself on an excellent memory, none of these men had worked together before. But there was a peculiar commonality. Sid had read the personnel records of every member of missile command. Every member of this crew had suffered a deep personal loss from an act of terrorism. Just like the colonel. What the hell?

This wasn't an accident, couldn't be an accident. What were they planning to do out there, say *Kaddish*, the prayer for the dead? Why there? Why on August 8? It was a puzzle, but Sid didn't see any way to solve it. He turned his attention back to his other tasks, but the problem ricocheted irritatingly around in his subconscious.

August 7, 5:00 P.M. IDT   ***Everywhere***

"In the name of Allah, the compassionate, the merciful…" The predictable formulaic introduction rolled out of television speakers tuned to news channels throughout Israel and the rest of the world. The Saudi Arabian government had scheduled an emergency announcement during evening news time in Israel, morning news time in Washington. That was unusual, and the electronic news media, CNN, Fox News, all of them, had scrambled to preempt their scheduled programming. Millions of television and computer screens around the world showed the Saudi defense minister, Prince Salman bin Talal, wearing not the blue pin-striped business suit he usually affected when addressing Western audiences, but classic Arab dress, white robes, the *kaffiyeh* headdress, everything.

"Our sacred role as the guardians of Mecca, the Holy City, is central to the domestic and foreign policy of the Kingdom of Saudi Arabia. To be a guardian, one must be not only vigilant, but also powerful, more powerful than any who might dare to threaten the heart of Islam. For many years, we have maintained an army and an air force equipped with the most modern planes and weapons that the wealth granted to us by Allah could obtain, every weapon imaginable, save one. We have not previously possessed nuclear weapons." He paused for effect, and his expression darkened. He leaned forward and his voice rose. "But that has now changed. Let everyone who contemplates attacking or even affronting us take warning. We are now in possession of nuclear bombs. We will no longer tolerate foreign interference in our affairs, or those of any Muslim country. We will respond to any attack on Islam, its people, its land, its symbols, with a mushroom cloud of annihilation. Take heed." He stepped back from the microphone, and the transmission ended.

August 7, 6 P.M. IDT   Jerusalem

Tomorrow was August 8, the first day of Ramadan. Colonel Zvi ben-Aryeh sat stolidly in a straight-backed chair at the table in the kitchen of his apartment, waiting for his team to assemble for their final preparatory meeting, to go over the operational details for the last time. On the table was a maroon accordion folder, its drawstring unwrapped from the anchoring loop. There was a large cardboard container of Starbucks coffee on the table, and a plate of poppy seed cookies. (Whenever Jews meet, for any occasion, a celebration, a day of mourning, whatever, they eat.) One by one, the men climbed the stairs, knocked on the door, poured a cup of coffee, picked up a cookie, and sat down silently on one of the straight-backed chairs, arranged around the table.

Colonel Zvi ben-Aryeh had heard the Saudi broadcast earlier in the day. So had the rest of his team. All Israelis are news junkies, not out of morbid fascination, but because they want to survive. The news tells them when a new terrorist alert has been raised, so they can head for the shelters. It tells them when a new terrorist attack has occurred, so they can check on their families. It tells them when a new politician has proposed a compromise with the Palestinians that will drive them from their homes. In Israel, the news is a matter of life and death.

The Colonel emptied the contents of the folder onto the table. It contained copies of the engineering drawings of the missile silo control room, and working drawings of the missile in position in the silo. As the Colonel opened his mouth to begin the briefing, he was immediately interrupted. The eight hundred pound gorilla in the room could no longer be ignored. Shimon Naphtali, the guidance system technician, voiced what was nagging at the mind of every member of the team. "What is the point of continuing this farce? You know what today's announcement by the Saudis means! If we go forward, the Saudis will destroy one of our cities, probably Tel Aviv. We must call everything off."

Ben-Aryeh's face had gone pale at Naphtali's outburst. Then his face turned crimson and he slammed his fist down on the table. "The announcement changes nothing!" he shouted, "We move forward! If the Saudis don't attack us today, someone else will attack us tomorrow! We have been over all this before. The Pakistanis already have nuclear weapons, and the Iranians can't be two months away. The rest of the Muslims are already lined up to shovel us into the ovens. The only difference between the Holocaust and now is that the ashes would be radioactive. We are finished, finished, finished unless we finish Islam first. Unless we cut out its heart. We can't kill them all, but we can kill their faith. What happened to us when the Romans destroyed the Second Temple? The heart went out of us. We wandered in the desert of foreign countries for almost two thousand years, reduced to a pathetic rabble living on sufferance, universally despised and persecuted. What do you think will happen when the Muslims' holiest symbol is reduced to smoking rubble, when Allah utterly fails them? They may at first be able to strike back at us reflexively. We can survive that. We have survived worse. But within weeks, they will fall apart. They will no longer be able to promise seventy-two virgins to welcome every martyr into heaven. The Arab street that provides the cannon fodder that sustains Hamas and Hezbollah will no longer believe in anything, and will not mindlessly hurl its children into useless suicide bombings and mass riots. The Arab Spring rioters will blame the Islamists and turn on them. The Muslim Brotherhood will collapse. Muslim society will degenerate into the traditional Arab cesspool of tribal warfare and sexual perversion. They will be powerless to threaten us any longer. Now, stop sniveling and let's get on with the job."

Leadership matters. It instills courage where only fear has existed before. Naphtali looked chastened, eyes downcast to the table. When he looked up, fire had returned to his eyes. "Of course, you're right. This is our only hope. Let us indeed get on with it." The team nodded their assent.

Colonel ben-Aryeh pushed the first of the control room drawings into the center of the table. Every man leaned forward to better see the picture. They were all familiar with the control room, but they also recognized that the success of their plan required automatic execution of all the requisite tasks, a result that could only be assured by repetitive reviews. They listened intently as the Colonel again outlined the actions that each man would execute, pointing at the drawings in turn to illustrate the route each man would take. The process was repeated with the working drawings of the missile. Finally, the briefing was complete.

The Colonel gathered up the papers and returned them to the folder, closing it and wrapping the drawstring back into place. He looked around the table, locking eyes with each man in turn. "We are ready," he said, "and future generations will look back on us as the saviors of the Jewish people. We continue the tradition of Joshua at Jericho, of the Maccabees, of the founders of our new country. We will prevail! Now, go home and get some sleep. I will see you all tomorrow morning."

August 7, 7:30 P.M. IDT   **Jerusalem**
Despite the fact that the children, one year old Devorah and two year old Shoshana, were running around the kitchen like maniacs, Nina had dinner under control. A bowl of Israeli salad, made up of finely chopped tomatoes and cucumbers mixed with olive oil and lemon juice, was already on the small dining table. A bowl of couscous and a plate of sliced zucchini were waiting on the side of the sink. Nina was just pulling a roasted chicken out of the oven when Sid came in, followed a few minutes later by David. Sid and Nina plopped the children into high chairs and the group sat down to dinner.

As they ate and talked about nothing in particular, Nina noticed that Sid was uncharacteristically quiet and abstracted. As the meal was coming to an end, Nina decided to address the issue directly. "You're awfully quiet tonight, Sid. What's going on?"

Sid hesitated. Did he really want to discuss his vague misgivings with his family? On the other hand, he needed to talk to somebody. Talking out loud often clarified his thinking, and he certainly didn't want to talk about his worry at work; if he was wrong, he would be permanently damaging the reputations of people who didn't deserve it. In a security sensitive environment, suspicions, once raised, never, ever go away. So it was keep quiet and continue to stew or talk now. Sid decided to talk.

"Something strange is happening at work. You know that part of my job is to keep track of all our personnel. Every week, a duty roster gets posted for each day at each of the major facilities we run. The personnel assigned for tomorrow to a facility up near Netanya make up a really odd group, not at all the kind of group we usually assign. And every member of that group has had a loved one killed or mutilated by a terrorist attack. And so has my boss, Colonel ben-Aryeh, who made these assignments. I can't imagine why he put these people together. Or why he set it up for tomorrow. Maybe I'm being paranoid, but it just doesn't feel right."

Nina probed a little. "Why are you worried? When I was on active duty in the Army, crazy stuff happened all the time. What kind of facility is it, anyway?"

"That's the problem," replied Sid. "It's not supposed to be generally known, but of course everybody does know. It's a missile launch complex."

Everyone became silent. The temperature in the room seemed to drop twenty degrees. "You're afraid that this is some kind of rogue operation to bomb the Arabs, aren't you?" Nina's face was white. "That's crazy! Why now, when there's actually a real chance for peace?"

"Because some people are crazy. They don't care about peace. They just want revenge."

David had a queer look on his face. "Jasmine mentioned to me that tomorrow is a Muslim holiday, the first day of Ramadan. Ramadan is just like *Yom Kippur*, the Day of Atonement when we fast and repent, only it lasts a month. She told me something very strange too. She had a bizarre conversation with one of her father's surgeons, a Dr. Musawi. She thought he wanted to talk with her about relief efforts for Lebanese children injured in border skirmishes. But it wasn't about that at all. He started talking vaguely about the need for some kind of major event, what he called 'facts on the ground,' to change the border situation. What he wanted to do was recruit her to explain the reasons the Arabs needed to take action when she got back to Columbia. And she said that she had gotten the impression he was talking about something that he knew would occur very soon."

Something clicked in Sid's head. Did Gradsteyn provide launch information to Arab fanatics? And if he did, when would they use it? On Ramadan? My God, do we have two sets of madmen getting ready to launch Armageddon tomorrow?

"I'm afraid I know what the doctor is talking about. We've had operational launch information and a guidance circuit board go missing. Security thinks that it was stolen by a sleazy industrial spy they picked up in a sting operation. But I don't think he had anything to do with it. And what you're telling me is that the information may now be in the hands of Islamic terrorists."

Nina was skeptical. "This is nonsense! You both have been reading too many cheap thrillers. Even if it were true, and it isn't, there's nothing you can do. Who would believe this story if you told it? What do you base it on? Some silly gossip from your cousin's girlfriend? A hunch that you know more than Dov Kavni, one of the best security officers in the Army? Come on, Sid!"

One great advantage of being young is the ability to jump to conclusions based on very few facts and to act on them with a complete disregard of the possible consequences. David leapt into the conversation. "You've got to go with your gut, Sid. Something very bad is about to happen and you're the only one who can stop it. What time does the new crew go on duty?"

"It's a twelve hour shift. The new crew goes on at 9:00 A.M."

"It's a two hour drive to Netanya. You're leaving here around 7:00 A.M. to be up there when the new crew comes on duty. I'll keep you company on the drive." It was not a suggestion. "And we'd better bring along some heavy artillery."

CHAPTER 10

C olonel Zvi ben-Aryeh sat at his kitchen table, drinking what he knew could be his last cup of coffee ever. Much to his surprise, he had slept soundly through the night, waking only when the alarm buzzer had gone off at six. He had rolled out of bed, showered, shaved, and put on a clean uniform. No sloppiness, no casualness. Today was a momentous day, and he felt it deserved respect.

The Chinese say that he who sets out on revenge should first dig two graves, he thought, and they have something there. When Mecca disappears in a blinding flash of light and a whirlwind of radioactive debris, the world will change forever. The Muslims will strike back, or at least attempt to strike back. Thank God for the Arrow anti-missile system! But no defensive system is perfect. Some of their attacks will get through. Perhaps one of them will get me. But it will be worth it.

He rose from the table and took a final look around the room. Memories of his dead wife and child flashed through his mind, thoughts of what might have been. He dismissed them and headed out. He trotted down the corridor, walked down the steps and out the door, climbed into his jeep and headed for the missile complex. He threaded his way through the city streets and took an on-ramp to Route 1. He put his foot down hard on the accelerator, coming rapidly to a speed of 150 kilometers per hour. The posted speed limit was 100 kilometers per hour. Israelis do not believe in speed limits.

August 8, 7:30 A.M. IDT   Jerusalem

Beneath the streets of the Old City, Musawi's Hamas cell prepared for the ultimate *jihad*. Musawi and his men sat around the long wooden table, nervously sipping their sweet, syrupy coffee from Styrofoam cups, all except Musawi who was drinking his usual mint tea. Musawi started the final briefing. "The missile complex will be most vulnerable an hour after the shift change. At that time, the new crew will have completed checking in with the central command, and they will be completely absorbed in running through missile status checks. They will not be monitoring the area outside the silo." He smiled slightly and pointed to the pile of photographs of manual pages pilfered for him by Gradsteyn. "The Israeli procedural manuals are quite detailed. There is no question that my description is correct. While the crew is too busy to be aware of anything other than the task at hand, we will strike."

One of his men had the temerity to question his timing. "We should attack immediately when the gate is opened for the new crew. It would be easier to get into the complex then." Musawi turned livid, jumped up from his chair, strode around the table and slapped him sharply across the face. "Never question any of my decisions again! I expect perfect discipline. Just do what you're told!" His anger released, Musawi relented slightly. "But to answer your objection, that would be a tactical error of the greatest magnitude. If we were to attack at that point, the noise would alert the crew still inside to the existence of a threat, and would give them enough time to access their weapons. When we forced the door, we would be met with fierce resistance. Worse, the crew would have time to summon reinforcements. We attack as I have planned." Musawi walked back to his chair and sat down. "We have had enough useless discussion. We will continue with the briefing."

Musawi reached below the table and retrieved a bag containing the eight melons brought from Lebanon by an unsuspecting Jasmine. He gently ran a knife blade around the circumference of each and pulled apart the two hemispherical melon shells, revealing six inch diameter spheres of a claylike substance. The cell clustered around Musawi. "These little balls are made of Semtex, the most powerful plastic explosive known to man. It makes the C-4 they smuggle from Gaza look like a firecracker. We will insert detonators into two of the balls and place them at the base of the fence posts on each side of the main gate. The explosion will blow the fence posts out of the ground and fling the gate a hundred yards out into the desert. We will then enter the station and place the six remaining balls around the main silo door. This explosion will blow off the door, and we will enter the silo. We will kill the men on duty and then get on with the job."

Musawi's men returned to their places around the table. Musawi reached under the table again, pulled out a black Halliburton attaché case, laid it on the table, and released the catches, which opened with a sharp snap. He lifted the lid and removed a circuit board. "This is the re-programmed on-board navigation and arming control. Our friend in the aerospace engineering department of the Technion, has set it to aim the missile at Tel Aviv, and to arm the warhead during its descent when it reaches an altitude of five hundred feet." He smiled again, more broadly this time. "It is wonderful that the Israelis have adopted the American idea of affirmative action. They have put Arabs into every technical and scientific department in the name of diversity. They have turned their Zionist institutions into daggers for us to plunge into their hearts. Fools! They deserve to die!" Musawi finished his gloating and returned to the operational plan. "Even with perfect timing, there is a possibility that we will meet with some resistance when we enter the silo. If we do, our first priority is to protect this circuit board until the resistance has been suppressed. As soon as we have complete control, we will open the launch tube access hatch marked on this diagram, enter the launch tube, open the access port in the missile and replace the circuit board. We will then reclose the port, exit the launch tube, close the access hatch, and launch the missile. And, *inshallah*, the doom of the Zionist entity will be sealed.

"We will then make our escape. We will have approximately ten minutes until the missile strikes Tel Aviv. In ten minutes, we will be well away from the missile complex and safe."

The men were breathing hard, the taste of victory already in their mouths. Musawi made it seem so certain, so easy. And even if he was wrong, even if they could not make their escape, they would die as *shahids*, as martyrs. *Allah akbar!* God is great! They rose from the table and climbed the stairs to the street and their waiting white minivan, loaded with weapons and destiny. It was 8:00 A.M.

August 8, 10:00 A.M. IDT   Near Netanya

Sid Goldman and David Hirsch bounced uncomfortably along in Sid's jeep. The seat was cramped. In addition to the two of them, it held a formidable array of firepower. Sid had brought his standard issue Uzi submachine gun. He had also stopped by the armory and drawn several additional weapons. He was a very persuasive guy, and it should have been a straightforward process since his credentials showed that he was assigned to a designated "dangerous area." But this was the army. It always takes an hour longer than you expect.

Sid had drawn a Desert Eagle Mark XIX 50AE pistol with a ten inch barrel holding seven cartridges as big as machine gun rounds. He had also drawn a B-300 rocket launcher, an Israeli developed anti-tank weapon. The U.S. army had adopted it to replace the venerable bazooka. It had taken a little persuasion to have the B-300 issued, but not much, since terrorist infiltrators were increasingly using lightly armored vehicles.

David had never seen a B-300 before. He was fascinated. "How does it work, Sid?" Despite the tension, Sid was amused. Boys like toys, he thought, especially toys that go bang. I'll give him a thirty second lesson. It will help keep his mind off the reality of what we may be up against. He took one hand off the steering wheel and pointed to the various parts of the weapon. "It's as easy to shoot as any other gun. You see that little canister on the floor? That's the rocket. You shove the canister into the back of the launcher. It has an arrow on it to make sure you don't put it in backwards. Then you lift the launcher onto your shoulder, take aim through the sight, and pull the trigger. The rocket shoots out the front at 400 miles per hour, and a blast of fire shoots out the back for 300 feet. Whatever the rocket hits just disappears." David gasped out the expected "Wow!" and leaned back in his seat.

They continued down the highway. As the time for action approached, David began to fidget nervously. Except for his initial flash of provocative bravado to prod Sid into action, David didn't have a clue what to do. His military background was nil. Firing a gun instinctively when your life was threatened was one thing. Determining tactics for a confrontation with potentially fanatical soldiers was another. "So, what do we do when we get there, Sid?"

Sid had been thinking hard about that. The kid had certainly gotten him up off his rear end and into action, but he knew that he could be wrong, even if the kid didn't. Coincidences do happen. Everybody in Israel has *some* personal connection to a terrorism tragedy.

"We've got to handle this very carefully until we know what's actually going on. You're going to stay out of sight in the jeep. I'm going to say that we're pulling a snap readiness inspection, I've got the authority to do that, and I'll go inside to look around. As soon as I'm done, I'll say that I'm finished and come out. It won't' take more than ten minutes. If I've seen anything fishy, if anyone acted unusually, I will call for a rapid reaction squad to get out here fast."

The jeep exited the highway and headed out onto the small road to the missile complex. The fenced compound was just coming into view.

August 8, 10:00 A.M. IDT   Near Netanya

The shift change at 9:00 A.M. had been uneventful. Colonel Zvi ben-Aryeh's men greeted their opposite numbers in the crew going off duty, then sat down at their assigned stations. Menachem Aronot, whose job as silo mechanic also gave him responsibility for physical security, limped over to a switch panel, tripped the fence gate release and watched the security system monitor while the intercom speakers blared out the whine of the gate motor and the rumble of car engines as the off duty crew got into their vehicles and exited, heading to their various homes for breakfast and sleep. When the last vehicle had left, he sent a routine confirmation of completion of the shift change at Launch Complex 4 over the secure link to the central command center in Jerusalem, but didn't close the gate. Ten minutes later, ben-Aryeh drove through the gate and entered the silo, carrying his old fashioned leather briefcase. Aronot closed the gate as ben-Aryeh swung the large lever which threw the security bolt on the door. Aronot then sent a second message to the central command center saying that they were experiencing a problem with the main power supply for the communications gear. Ten minutes later, he sent another message saying that they had located the problem, but that they had to shut down communications for about ninety minutes to make the necessary repairs. Launch Complex 4 was now essentially isolated.

"All right, we're ready to go!" shouted ben-Aryeh. "Even if, God forbid, we trip an alarm, central command will think it's just due to the power supply repairs. Even if they are a little suspicious, they will twiddle their thumbs for an hour and a half waiting for voice communications to come back up so they can ask what the hell is going on. After all, what's an hour and a half? Now, move!"

The control room erupted into activity. Aronot grabbed a socket wrench from the emergency toolkit stored beneath the launch officer's desk and quickly removed the six bolts securing the cover panel for the alarm system. He clipped jumper wires across the leads from the sensors on the silo access door in the rear wall, ensuring that no tell-tale current interruptions would occur when the access doors were opened. "Access door alarm safe," he shouted. He then scampered across the room, amazingly fast for an old man with a limp, broke the access door seals, and practically dived through. He clambered up the ladder leading to the weather doors, bypassed the door alarm, and waited. Jonah Fischman and Avram Gush followed close behind.

Fischman climbed up to open the warhead hatch on the side of the missile. He carefully removed the standard arming device which needed an alphabet soup of security codes sent by the defense minister and the president to activate the warhead, and replaced it with his own arming device, which decidedly did *not* need any codes from politicians to arm the bomb. He stared at the bomb, still merely an inert conglomeration of metal assemblies and electronic parts, and was surprised to find tears running down his cheeks. "How can I kill so many people?' he thought, "people I don't even know, people who don't care about politics, people who are innocent?" And then he thought of his dead wife, of the school full of dead children. "Innocent like hell! You dance in the streets when Jews die. The Torah says you should not commit murder, but it sure doesn't say you cannot kill. It says you *should* kill to save a life. How many Jewish lives are we saving? Millions! How can I kill you, you murderous Islamic animals? Like this!" and he threw the activating lever and climbed back down the ladder. The bomb was now set to detonate when the accelerometer indicated that the missile was on a downward trajectory and the altimeter indicated that it had descended to an altitude of one thousand feet. This detonation profile both assured the vaporization of everything directly below the explosion, and also guaranteed a tremendous shockwave that would destroy anything, and any person, within a mile. The explosion would occur directly above the Kaaba, the ancient building which is the central shrine of Islam.

Gush climbed down to the exhaust nozzles. He disconnected the safety interlocks on the solid fuel igniters, and bypassed the ignition sequencer so that it was directly connected to the master launch switch. He looked at his work with satisfaction. "So, you *mamserim*, you bastards, you killers of my family! See how you like it when your whole goddamned world dies!" He spat on the floor and climbed back up.

Ben-Aryeh opened his briefcase and took out the Mecca guidance chip, carefully packed into an anti-static plastic case, and handed it to Shimon Naphtali. Naphtali walked calmly across the floor to the main guidance computer cover panel, opened the latch, and lowered the panel on its hinges to a horizontal position. He touched the panel to discharge any static electricity that might have accumulated on his body, then reached for the chip remover held by a small clip in the panel corner. He deftly extracted the original targeting chip and inserted the Mecca chip. He thought of his young wife and her shredded womb, of the children they would never have, and felt an emptiness that would never go away. "This will not make us even, you Muslims and me. I will never be made whole. But, by God, you will never be able to destroy any of us again." He closed the panel.

It was almost done. So far, nothing was visible from outside the silo. Ben-Aryeh signaled Aronot to open the weather doors. As they opened, Aronot hurried down the ladder and climbed through the access door into the control room. Ben-Aryeh and his team knew that they had only a few minutes left to complete the plan. Six hundred miles above them, keyhole satellites would detect the opening and flash warning signals to capitals around the world, including Jerusalem. A commando team would soon be speeding toward Launch Complex 4.

But there was time for last words. "We have done it, my friends. When we complete the launching procedure, Islam will enter its death throes. You can all be proud of what we have done." And then the floor shook and they heard the roar of the first explosion.

August 8, 10:00 A.M. IDT   Near Netanya

Hussein Musawi and his men parked their van about one hundred yards away from the gate of Launch Complex 4. Two men piled out of the vehicle, dragging a green steel ammunition box mounted on a skateboard. They scurried up to the gate, packed Semtex around the posts which supported the gate at either side, inserted timed detonators set for sixty seconds, and ran back to the van.

The explosion cut through the gateposts like a band saw. The posts, the gate and part of the fence flew into the air, and one side of the fence collapsed into a tangle of chain link wreckage. The van raced forward over the now flattened fence and stopped fifty feet in front of the silo door. The same two men again jumped out of the van and packed Semtex all around the control room entrance door, again inserted detonators, and ran back to the van. The second explosion sliced through the locking bolt and ripped the door off its hinges, flinging it to the ground. As the smoke cleared, Musawi's men, each carrying an AK-47, leapt out of the van and rushed down the stairs. Musawi followed carrying the Halliburton attaché case containing the guidance computer circuit board programmed for Tel Aviv.

August 8, 10:06 A.M . IDT   Near Netanya

Ben-Aryeh and his men were technicians, true, but they were soldiers first. The fact that you are in charge of a nuclear bomb doesn't mean that you don't have other weapons at your disposal. Launch Complex 4, like every other launch complex, had a small arms locker. At the sound of the first explosion, every man sprinted to the locker, grabbed an Uzi and a handful of ammunition clips, dived for cover behind the nearest desk or equipment rack, and focused his attention on the entrance stairway. By the time Musawi and his men set off the explosives that breached the door, ben-Aryeh and his men had established a defensive position. They were ready when the Arabs cascaded down the stairs.

August 8, 2:00 A.M. EDT   Langley, Virginia

The KH-12 Keyhole satellite swam silently through the vacuum of space, scanning the Israeli desert. It beamed real-time images from its high resolution cameras to a U.S. Department of Defense relay station in Cyprus that forwarded it to CIA headquarters in Langley, Virginia. The images were fed simultaneously to the super-computers of the National Geo-Spatial Intelligence Agency, where the images were analyzed by a sophisticated pattern recognition software program that identified changes from images collected in earlier passes over the same location. The change at the location of Launch Complex 4 triggered a Level 1 warning popup on the screen of one of the technicians monitoring the satellite feed. The screen was a maze of rarely changing numbers reporting the health of the satellite and its onboard equipment.

Tim Conrad sat in front of the screen, leaning back in his chair with his feet propped on the desk. He was wearing an open necked sport shirt and worn jeans, the mandatory holes in the knees. Tim was bored. Working the graveyard shift was always boring. He had eaten a large sausage and pepperoni pizza before coming on duty at midnight, and he felt a little sluggish. The popup was interesting, but certainly not worrisome. It broke the monotony. Level 1 warnings appeared all the time. They were always trivial. Maybe a flock of birds had landed. Maybe someone was walking around. Who knew? He flipped a switch, and the numbers vanished from the screen and were replaced by the direct video feed, which showed a picture of the top of the missile silo with the doors open.

Conrad's feet came off the desk with a bang. This was way out of the ordinary. Grabbing the telephone on his desk, he dialed the alert code and was instantly connected to the head of the image interpretation division. "Bill, this is Tim Conrad. There is something weird going on. Pull my screen up." Bill Rutledge sighed. The new kids always got their panties in a knot when they saw something new. "Take it easy, Tim, I'll take a look. It's probably nothing." He pulled the image up on the 50 inch LCD panel that filled one wall of his office. "OK, Tim, I see it. I'll get the operational people on this immediately." He hung up the phone and hesitated for a minute. The last thing he needed was to get a reputation as a Nervous Nellie. Bill was 57, overweight and hypertensive. He didn't want his bald head and thick glasses relegated to a tiny cubicle reserved for over-the-hill analysts. But sometimes you have to take the risk. For something like this, you don't go through channels. He picked up the phone again and dialed the emergency code. The line was picked up immediately by the duty officer at the critical threat desk. "Go!" barked a voice. Bill steadied his voice and panted "We have a possible impending missile launch at one of the Israeli launch sites."

Military and intelligence services spend every waking moment establishing protocols for every conceivable circumstance. Because Israel was a U.S. ally, the protocol in this case included immediately contacting the duty officer's opposite number in Israel to ask what was going on. There was the possibility that the satellite had merely detected a routine test of the silo equipment, although he would have expected to have received advance notification, to avoid precisely the flap that was going on now. The duty officer typed out a quick description of the situation and shot it out over the secure link to the Israeli military.

August 8, 10:10 A.M *. IDT*   *Jerusalem*

A klaxon horn suddenly shattered the calm of the central missile command operations room in Jerusalem. No explanation was needed – that horn meant only one thing. A nuclear missile was about to be launched. Satellite detection of the unscheduled opening of the weather doors on the Launch Complex 4 silo had initiated a response protocol which had been in place for years, but had never been expected to be used. Central command had lost control of a nuclear missile.

Major Shlomo Einstein had been in charge of the night shift, and his relief was an hour and ten minutes overdue. He was tired, he needed a shave, he needed sleep, and now he was the man in charge in the middle of a major emergency. Where the devil was ben-Aryeh? He was due in at 9:00 and he was never late. Except today. Major Einstein felt sweat accumulating in his armpits, and saw his hands beginning to shake. "Pull yourself together!" he thought. "Do your job!" The shaking stopped.

And in the middle of this mess, communications with the site were down. Something about a power supply problem. He knew it wouldn't work, but he gave the order anyway. "Execute a master override on Launch Complex 4. Shut it down!" The Lieutenant at the control console lifted a plastic switch cover and smashed his fist down on a large red spring loaded button. "Major, we're not getting the shutdown completion acknowledgement signal. They're still running." Not good.

Israel is constantly under attack. Hamas shooting rockets from Gaza in the west, Hezbollah shooting rockets from the north, snipers, infiltrators in jeeps, always something. So the Israeli Defense Forces specialize in rapid response. Every hour of every day, there are units on alert, ready to saddle up at a moment's notice. Einstein needed one of them now.

Crazy ideas swirled through Einstein's head. What was happening? Arab terrorists seizing the complex? Rogue military with some incomprehensible agenda? Extortionists, like something out of a James Bond novel? Or just a simple mechanical failure, terrifying but in the end harmless? He picked up a phone with a direct link to Colonel Aaron Livni, the commanding officer of the unit tasked with supporting central missile command, a line that was constantly monitored by the office of the Minister of Defense, and shouted "This is Einstein. There is a problem at Launch Complex 4. The silo doors have just had an unscheduled opening. We've lost our communications link, and the remote shutdown procedure has failed. We don't know what's going on. We need the team out there now!" Livni didn't waste any time. "We're on our way," he said, and hung up. He hit the scramble siren, and ran toward a waiting helicopter, followed by the ready crew. In fifteen seconds they were airborne and heading out over the desert.

August 8, 2:10 A.M. EDT   ***Washington, D.C.***

The satellite detection of the opening of the weather doors on Launch Complex 4 triggered DefCon 4, the highest level of U.S. preparedness for war. President Lippincott sat unhappily in the War Room beneath the White House. It was the middle of the night, and he was lucky that he could assemble Secretary of Defense Howard and the heads of the CIA and the DIA. There wasn't time to wait for anybody else to be located and called in.

Lippincott didn't waste any words. "We have just detected the opening of the doors on an Israeli nuclear missile silo. Those insane Israelis are going to attack Iran. And what happens next? The Republican Guard invades Iraq. We shoot at them. The crazy Saudis shoot at us. The entire world dissolves in radioactive flame. So we stop it, and we stop it now. The Israeli prime minister is being called to the phone, and I will spend thirty seconds trying to talk some sense into his arrogant head. If that is not effective, if we don't see those doors close, we will shoot a nuclear-tipped cruise missile down that silo."

A light flashed on the red telephone and the President pushed a button connecting the phone to the sound system which covered the entire room. Before Prime Minister Sorkin could say a word, the President launched into his Jeremiad. "We have detected the opening of the weather doors on one of your nuclear missile silos, from which we conclude that you are about to launch a pre-emptive attack on Iran. We have discussed this before, and you know our position. We have no time for further discussion. We are not going to allow your paranoia to destroy the world. Shut that missile down immediately, or we will do it for you. We have a nuclear missile of our own targeted on the site right now. You have ten seconds to answer."

Sorkin paused before answering. "Mr. President, believe me, we are not attacking Iran. We do not intend to attack Iran. We have had a small problem with the control system for the weather doors on one silo, and we are in the process of fixing it. Your attack on the silo would be pointless. We will let you know as soon as the problem is fixed. We were in the process of alerting your government when I received this call. Please don't threaten us again before you have all the facts, Mr. President. We are your firmest friends and a loyal ally. Goodbye, Mr. President." The phone went dead.

The War Room was silent. Maybe I have too itchy a trigger finger, thought the President. In Jerusalem, Jacob Sorkin took a deep breath. I am undoubtedly the best liar on the planet, he thought. Thank God.

August 8, 10:10 A.M. IDT   Near Netanya

Sid and David arrived at the complex to see Musawi and his men streaming into the silo. Sid rammed the jeep through the wreckage of the fence and screeched to a stop near the entrance. Shouting "David! Stay here and keep your head down!" he grabbed his Uzi, dropped to his belly, and crawled over to look inside.

The scene was like every other battle; a combination of a fireworks display and a butcher shop. Musawi's men were fanatics, but they were also amateurs. Spinning like a whirling Dervish with your AK-47 on full automatic is not effective unless you're shooting at unarmed civilians. John Wesley Hardin, the greatest gunfighter of the American Old West, was once asked his advice on how to win a gun fight. His answer was "Take your time, and don't miss." That's what professionals do, and Israeli soldiers are professionals. The first two terrorists down the stairs were dead before their feet hit the floor, bullets through their heads. Blood and brains spattered the walls.

But terrorists are neither stupid nor inflexible. The remaining men halted their headlong rush, and took advantage of the fact that, being at the top of the stairs, they held the high ground. The desks and racks which the defenders were using for cover provided little protection from an attack from above. Musawi's remaining men switched their AK-47's to semi-automatic and began firing individual shots, aiming carefully at each of the defenders inside and then huddling back against the stairwell wall.

Musawi kept to the rear, holding the precious briefcase with the Tel Aviv circuit board in a death grip and shielding it with his body. To his surprise, he was not in the least frightened, even though this was his first time in actual combat. He knew that Allah favored his cause, and that the resistance by the Jews, while unanticipated, would be short-lived.

Ben-Aryeh knew all about combat, so he *was* frightened. If you're not frightened in combat, you are either stupid or crazy. In either case, you're dead. But his fear was not for his own life. It was that his mission might fail. He looked over to the firing switch. He wanted to spring over and throw it, but if he broke cover he knew he would be cut to pieces before he reached it. He would have to wait until the battle was resolved, one way or the other.

August 8, 10:12 A.M . IDT   Near Netanya

Riding in a helicopter is like being in a falling elevator attached to a bumper car containing a chainsaw. The noise is deafening and the motion is nauseating. The commando team didn't really notice. As the Bell UH-1 Iroquois "Huey" helicopter whumped across the desert, Colonel Livni braced himself against a strut and leaned forward to shout instructions to his team. "OK, listen up! We don't know how much time we have, or exactly what we're up against. We do know that there is a chance that someone is attempting to launch the missile. If they are, once that missile leaves the silo and gets up to speed, it doesn't matter what we do. Somewhere, there's going to be a nuclear explosion and the world will never be the same. We need to get inside fast and prevent a launch if that's what is being attempted. It's like a hostage rescue situation: hit them before they know they've been hit. We blow the door and throw flash-bang grenades down the stairs to disorient everyone inside. Then we pile in and shoot anything that moves."

Livni then turned away from his men and pulled on the communications headset that was live to central missile command. His next comments were not for the men, who were studying a blueprint of the complex, and planning tactics that would let them avoid getting killed during the operation. "We're almost at the site, Einstein. Now you need to tell me whether there is any way we will set that goddamned bomb off." Strangely, it was an easy question, even if it had an unpleasant answer. "Not that I know of," replied Einstein, "but I can't be sure. If the missile hasn't been meddled with, there's no problem. It's not like a stick of dynamite. Setting it off is a complex process, and hitting it with a sledge hammer or shooting it won't do anything. But if whoever's in there has altered the arming device, I don't know what can happen." He paused, and his voice took on an ironic tone. "But don't worry. If you set it off, you won't feel a thing."

Livni grunted and returned to his men. As the helicopter came in sight of Launch Complex 4, they saw the wreckage of the fence, the gaping hole where the control room door was supposed to be, and heard the unmistakable sound of small arms fire. What the hell? As von Clausewitz said, no battle plan survives first contact with the enemy.

August 8, 10:15 A.M. IDT   Near Netanya

Sid Goldman pulled back from the silo entrance as he heard the whine of ricochets from the walls. He couldn't do any good diving into the silo. He didn't even have any idea of who to shoot at if he did. What he needed was real combat support. He rolled further away from the door, pulled a military cell phone from his shirt pocket, and punched in an emergency code. The phone shifted to an encrypted mode and dialed the critical emergency station in central command. The phone was answered instantly. "This is Captain Sid Goldman. I am outside the silo at Launch Complex 4. The fence and the silo door have been breached, and there is an active firefight inside. I don't know who is in there, but there is a strong possibility that there are both terrorists and rogue army personnel involved. The weather doors are open. Someone intends to launch the missile. We need a combat team out here now."

"We read you, Captain. We are already aware that there is a situation, and we have a commando team on the way. Stand by." That's the army, thought Sid, stand by while the world blows up. He glanced over at the jeep. At least David is keeping his head down, he thought. He started crawling back to the jeep and had almost reached it when a round screamed up the staircase, ricocheted off the transom of the doorway, and slammed into his back. Sid screamed and passed out.

David heard the scream and peeked out the side of the jeep. He saw Sid face down in the sand, with a red stain covering his right shoulder and spreading down his back. David wriggled out the jeep door and pulled Sid to the side away from the silo door. David had no idea what to do for a bullet wound. All he knew about medicine he had learned from television shows. So what did they do on TV? Put pressure on the wound, I guess, he thought. He pulled off his shirt and shoved it inside Sid's jacket, then put his hand over the middle of the bloody area and pushed down.

Sid's eyes fluttered open as he returned to consciousness. He felt the pressure on his back, and turned his head to see a white-faced David hovering over him. "What are you doing, David?" "I think I'm stopping the bleeding. You're supposed to put pressure on a wound, right?" Boy, thought Sid, this kid can keep his head no matter what happens. "Right, but you can't hold that plug forever. So now I want you to turn me onto my back. My weight will keep enough pressure on." Sid groaned and gritted his teeth as David rolled him over, then closed his eyes and waited for the pain to subside. As soon as the pain had diminished enough to allow him to think, Sid began sketching out a strategy.

"Look, David, I don't know exactly who's in there, but whoever they are, they're crazy men. There's help on the way, but that missile could be launched at any minute. If help doesn't arrive soon, we're all that stands in the way of a nuclear catastrophe. Pull that B-300 launcher and the rocket round out of the jeep." He waited while David reached over the rocker panels and dragged them out. "Insert the rocket into the launcher and throw that safety lever off." David did. "Now, I'm going to take that launcher, crawl over to the silo weather doors, shove the launcher into the hole and blow up the missile." Sid paused for breath and reached weakly for the launcher.

David felt his heart start to pound. "That's impossible, Sid. If the missile is hit by a B-300 rocket that will set off the nuclear bomb, won't it?" Sid was getting weaker by the minute, but he managed to croak out "A nuclear bomb can't be set off that way. All that will happen is that it will become a pile of radioactive junk." David tried to absorb that idea. So it wasn't impossible to blow the missile up. But that meant only one thing. David swallowed hard. "Number two, Sid, you're in no shape to crawl six feet, let alone over to the silo weather doors. I'll do it." Sid started to protest, but David cut him off. "What other choice do we have? What does Hillel say? If not me, who?" Who indeed? thought David. If I get out of this alive, it will be a miracle. He grabbed the B-300 and crawled toward the silo.

August 8, 10:15 A.M . IDT   Near Netanya

The battle inside the silo was drawing to an end. One after another, the attackers and defenders cried out and fell, writhing out their last breaths in agony. Ben-Aryeh and Musawi were the only ones left. Musawi leaned quickly into the stairwell, but received no defensive fire. So, they are finally all dead, the Jews. It is our victory, and their finish. He moved away from the wall and walked confidently downstairs.

Ben-Aryeh prepared for the final action. It would only take a minute to run across the room and launch the missile. All he needed to do was get past this terrorist thug. He exploded out of hiding, heading for the launching switch. Musawi dropped his briefcase and tackled ben-Aryeh before he could reach it, and wrapped his hands around ben-Aryeh's throat. Ben-Aryeh threw himself backwards, broke Musawi's grip, and turned to break his neck. But Musawi grabbed him by the throat again, his desperation giving him preternatural strength. They rolled around on the floor, hands around each other's throats, until they were jammed against the launch control panel. Ben-Aryeh let go with his right hand, reached up, and threw the launching switch. The solid fuel rockets fired. Because the access doors had never been closed, the fiery exhaust filled the control room, incinerating Musawi, ben-Aryeh, and the remains of their men.

A nuclear bomb was on its way to Mecca.

CHAPTER 11

August 8, 10:15 A.M . IDT   *Near Netanya*

T he Huey slowed for the landing at Launch Complex 4. The commandos made another check of their gear. Colonel Livni gave them their final instructions. "The word is fast, fast, fast. Don't wait, don't think, just fire. Anything you see is to be considered a hostile, and on this one we do not take prisoners." But just as he finished speaking, a plume of flame erupted from the silo at Launch Complex 4. Livni and his men watched in stunned silence.

August 8, 10:16 A.M . IDT   Near Netanya
David heard the roar as the solid fuel motors ignited, and saw flame erupt from the weather doors. He saw the nose of the missile rising out of the silo. No time to shoot into the silo now, he thought, there's only time for one thing. As the missile rose into the air, David shouldered the B-300. It's just like shooting skeet, it's just like shooting skeet, he told himself, lead the target a little, not too much, God, I hope this acts like a shotgun, and he pulled the trigger. Time seemed to stop. The B-300 blowback

shrieked, the rocket leapt forward, the missile continued to rise, accelerating every microsecond. David held his breath. Will the rocket catch it? Will it?

The rocket struck the missile just above the exhaust nozzles, shearing them off, and igniting secondary fires along the length of the fuel chamber. David dropped to the ground and covered his head, still grasping the B-300. The missile's fuel supply exploded in a burst of flame, and fragments of the missile and the still intact warhead rained on the ground. The warhead thudded dully on the sand, its case a maze of dents and scratches. What had Sid said? Radioactive junk.

The helicopter lurched as the shock wave from the explosion reached it. The pilot pulled back sharply on the collective and the chopper rose rapidly, giving crew and passengers a good look at the complex. There wasn't much to see besides the wreckage, just two figures, one next to a jeep, one sitting on the ground with one hand curled around the handle of a B-300. The helicopter circled and came in for a landing.

The commandos piled out of the helicopter door, rifles at the ready. The assault squad, headed by Livni, ran to the control room door opening and rushed inside. They could see at a glance that the piles of ashes inside were no threat to anyone, not any more. Livni squawked "Clear" over the open channel, and the group climbed back out of the ruined silo. As the tension wound down, Livni took his first careful look around the site. The usual personal vehicles of an on-duty silo crew were parked nearby, but one vehicle was very much out of charac-ter. There was a white van parked inside the perimeter defined by the ruined fence. Grabbing two of his team, he walked over to the van. The sliding side door was open, and he could see pamphlets strewn across the floor. He reached in and picked one up. The cover showed a sketch of a Palestinian fighter, complete with *kaffiyeh*, holding a rifle aloft in the standard posture of defiance. Livni's Arabic was good enough for him to translate the caption emblazoned above the picture: "Liberate Our Land from the Infidels!" So, one set of shooters was Islamic terrorists. Livni walked around to the rear of the van to read the license plate, then pulled out his field communicator and called in the plate number to central command.

Livni and his men then headed to the jeep with Sid lying next to it. One of the men shouted over the open channel that he had an army officer with a serious bullet wound. One of the commandos sprinted back to the helicopter and returned with the emergency medical kit. He cut off Sid's jacket and applied a field dressing to the wound. Sid tried to smile. The commando squatted down beside him. "Glad to see you're alive," said Livni, "We knew you were here, and when we saw the mess, we figured you were dog meat. Do you know what happened?" Sid, face twisted with pain, shook his head. "I heard small arms fire and took a quick look into the control room, but all I saw were muzzle flashes and some blood spatter. I was crawling back toward the jeep when a ricochet caught me in the back. David pulled me back to cover behind the jeep." Sid leaned his head back with exhaustion, then continued "We knew that some maniac was going to try to launch the missile. We had to do something. I wanted to destroy it while it was still in the silo, but I didn't have the strength to crawl over to the weather doors dragging the B-300. So David grabbed the B-300 and headed over, but he didn't have time to get to the silo before the missile took off. I

don't see how he could do it, but the kid shot it down."
The commando looked at Sid strangely. "The kid shot it
down," he repeated, shaking his head in disbelief. But
he couldn't think about that now. He patted Sid on the
shoulder. "OK, that's enough for now. There's a medical
helicopter on the way. We'll take it from here." He rose
and walked back to the helicopter, muttering quietly to
himself, "I don't believe it. The kid shot it down?"

David sat on the ground. None too gently, one of the
men shouted at him "You don't belong on this base, kid!
What the hell are you doing here?" David stared back at
him. He thought of giving a long explanation. But he was
still a college kid, and no college kid could possibly resist
a once in a lifetime opportunity to be a heroic smartass.
"Saving the world, man," he replied "saving the world."
After all, it was true.

August 8, 7:30 P.M. IDT   Jerusalem

Properly bandaged, Sid Goldman hobbled into the top
security debriefing room in the Knesset building. It was
not what he had expected. It was set up like a court-
room, with a small table facing a curved dais. David was
already there, sitting at the table. There was an empty
chair next to him, and it was clear that Sid was to occupy
it. He sat down and looked at his interrogators. Not the
usual suspects. Sid recognized the head of missile command, no surprise there, the military police thunderbolt
Dov Kovni, and the heads of Mossad (the Israeli CIA)
and Shin Bet (internal security). But there were also the
Minister of Defense, and, good God, the Prime Minister!

The Prime Minister spoke first. "This is not the usual kind of debriefing, Captain Goldman and Mr. Hirsch," said Jacob Sorkin, "where we ask you questions and you give us answers. This debriefing is going to be inside out. We will give you answers, and you will be able to ask questions." He smiled. "Like 'Jeopardy' on American television. So, why are we doing this? Because what has happened could have unimaginable repercussions, for Israel, for the United States, for the Islamic world, and," his face becoming very stern, even threatening, "for both of you personally."

"First, let me tell you what actually happened. As you suspected, Captain Goldman, a rogue group of missile command personnel, every one the victim of a terrorist atrocity, determined to take revenge for their losses. Their method was to be the nuclear obliteration of the town of Mecca, carrying out the act on the first day of Ramadan." He paused to let that sink in. "It takes no imagination to predict what the consequences of such an action would be. Israel would be attacked by every Muslim state, not just the Arabs but the Pakistanis, the Indonesians, the Turks, the Iranians, the Somalis, the Nigerians, the Malaysians, and the recently nuclear armed Saudis. America would abandon us. We could not defend ourselves using conventional weapons, so we would use nuclear weapons. We would, because the alternative would be annihilation. And as soon as we detonated the first nuclear weapon, the Russians would come to the aid of their client states and obliterate us with nuclear weapons of their own. Then the U.S. Congress, stampeded by a few eloquent hotheads, would force America to attack Russia. Civilization, all civilization, would end." Sorkin paused again. He wiped his damp forehead with a handkerchief, took a drink of water, and then continued.

"But more was under way than The Mecca Plan, as the label we have put on the file containing all the information on this incident calls it. Jews do not have a monopoly on insanity. A Hamas cell here in Jerusalem successfully bribed an IDF staff sergeant to provide them with the schematic diagrams and operating manuals for the missile in Launch Complex 4. They then had an Arab engineering professor at the Technion, so much for diversity, create a special guidance circuit board for the missile. The target was Tel Aviv." Another long pause. "The consequences for the world would have been the same, the same sequence of attack and counter-attack ending in ultimate destruction.

"Neither plan succeeded, entirely because of the two of you. Israel owes you a great debt, America owes you a great debt, the world owes you a great debt. You deserve medals, parades, adulation by every person on the planet. But you won't get them."

Sid's face took on a resigned look. He had expected this, of course. But David looked dumbfounded. He blurted out "But why?"

Sorkin sighed. *He's too young to learn so much about the way the world really works. But he must.* "Because, David, none of this ever happened. Think about it. If the Islamic world gains any inkling of how close they came to suffering the ultimate sacrilege, our new peace deal will fall apart, and the Arabs will never again consider making peace with us, not for ten thousand years, if then. If the Palestinians learn that a tiny Hamas cell managed to gain access to one of our nuclear missiles, there will be a hundred, a thousand attacks on our missile sites, and one of them will succeed. If the Americans learn that our vaunted security is imperfect, that we cannot maintain absolute control over our nuclear weapons, they will do everything in their power to castrate us. They will cease military collaboration, they will join our enemies in UN votes of condemnation, they might, God forbid, strike an alliance with Iran. So this incident never occurred."

The head of Mossad spoke next. "There will be no newspaper coverage, no blogs, no rumors, nothing at all. Every military person who has had any contact with this operation will keep his mouth shut. And so will you, David. You will say nothing to your family, your friends, your lover, anyone else you know. You may mention it to God on Yom Kippur, the Day of Atonement, but you will do it silently. If we have any indication that you are about to break your silence, our people, and we have people everywhere, will silence you. Permanently."

David was incredulous. Kill me? Heroic little me? But this was crazy. David started shaking with anger. "You can't cover this up! The U.S. knows where all your missile sites are. Spy satellites watch everything that happens at every one of them! They must have seen the explosions! It will all come out, whether I talk about it or not!"

The Minister of Defense had grandchildren about David's age. He liked them, and he liked David. He admired their enthusiasm, he applauded their direct-ness. He celebrated David's bravery and skill. So he broke in gently. "You're partially right, David. Something will come out, but it will be a little different from what you expect. Let me tell you what is going to happen. In about two weeks, there is going to be a reception for several Congressmen and their staffs at the Israeli embassy in

Washington. The embassy personnel at the reception will include our military attaché. He is going to have a little too much to drink, and he will let slip that we had a problem at one of our non-existent missile sites. It seems that we had installed a new type of nozzle controller on one of our missiles, one we had purchased from an American manufacturer. I suppose we should have bought Japanese. Anyhow, it was defective, and during a routine test it ignited a fuel section and we had to use the missile's self-destruct mechanism to prevent an unintended launch. We are still cleaning up the mess. And that will be that."

David was unsatisfied. "Nobody will believe that."

"You are wrong, David. Everybody will believe it. It is the most convenient thing to believe. It isn't threatening, it isn't frightening, it is exactly the kind of thing that happens in the ordinary course of events. So why not believe it."

"And what about the families of the soldiers who were killed? What do you tell them? And what happens when the Arabs disappear?"

"We tell the families of the soldiers that they were killed in a training accident. We offer our condolences. We have military funerals, we will say the *Kaddish*, the prayer for the dead, and the soldiers will be remembered as heroes who died to protect the Jewish people.

"And as for the terrorists? Terrorists come and go. We will put out a story that another group of Palestinians has headed off to Afghanistan to carry out *jihad*. It was probably the missing men. So everything is tied up in a neat little bundle."

David slumped in his chair. Sid put an arm around his shoulders, leaned over, and whispered "Don't feel too bad, David. That's the way things are always done. Welcome to the big leagues."

Prime Minister Jacob Sorkin got up from his chair, walked around the dais, and came up to Sid and David. Sid and David rose automatically. Sorkin put out his hand, shaking hands first with Sid. "Captain, you are an extraordinary officer. You have great perception and exceptional courage. You have a brilliant career ahead of you, I guarantee you of that, and it is my privilege to know you." He then turned to David and extended his hand. "Young man, you are one in a million, in a hundred million. You have indeed saved the world, as you said." David blushed, but Sorkin's eyes twinkled. "It's all right, you should be proud of yourself. One of our greatest Prime Ministers, Golda Meir, had a saying: 'Don't be modest. You're not that great.' But you are going to need to be modest. The safety of the world depends on it. I know you're up to it." He released David's hand and turned to leave. Over his shoulder, he said "Have a safe trip home, David, and be careful when you get there. New York is a dangerous place."

August 9, 9:00 A.M . IDT   **Jerusalem**
A much chastened Herman Schneiderman was once again sitting in the interrogation room. His time in the slammer had not been kind to him. He was cold, he was dirty, he needed a shave, his clothes were rumpled, and he smelled bad. He squirmed in his chair.

Behind the one-way glass, Dov Kovni examined him like a bug under a microscope. He is fully cooked, he thought to himself. Time to finish this up. Kovni left the observation booth, entered the main room, and pounced without any preamble.

"You don't look so good after a couple of days in prison, Schneiderman. How do you think you'll look after thirty years? Because that's what you're looking at, you miserable little schmuck. Espionage, attempted theft of government secrets, those aren't just parking tickets. We dropped the murder charge, it turns out that it was somebody else, so you won't get fifty years. But thirty years is still a fair amount of time. And I will guarantee that it will be hard time, as you say in America."

Schneiderman turned white. His mind spun wildly. *Thirty years! And I'm supposed to be relieved because it isn't fifty years? Are you kidding me? I'll be seventy-five when I get out, if I live that long. I won't even be able to get it up! Jesus Christ!* But before his thoughts got completely out of control, his professional cunning reasserted itself. *Don't panic, boy, he thought, he has a reason for telling you this. He's not just scaring you shit-less to try to get a plea bargain. He doesn't need one. He has me cold. He wants something. This is a negotiation.*

The color returned to Schneiderman's face. He looked straight back at Kovni. "All right. I'm looking at thirty years. I don't want to do thirty years. But *you* don't want me to do thirty years either, or you wouldn't be here. So what do you propose we do?"

Kovni pretended to think, gnawing his lower lip and staring down at the table. He raised his eyes slowly. "Schneiderman, you are not the only slime ball slithering around stealing industrial and defense secrets. We have our own slime balls, too. And we would really like to have one based in America, with an American address, and an American passport, and an American accent. So we are going to do one of two things. One, we can let you rot in prison for thirty years, and we will make them the most horrible years you can imagine. Or, two, you are going to go to work for us. These are the terms of your employment. You will steal what we tell you to steal. You will sell what we tell you to sell. You can keep your apartment and your girlfriends. The first time you try to cross us, we blow your brains out. What's your choice?"

Not too bad, thought Schneiderman, not too bad at all.

August 9, 11:00 A.M . IDT   Jerusalem

"So you won't tell me where you've been." Jasmine pouted as she and David walked along Jerusalem's Ben Yehudah Street in the warm morning sunshine, holding hands and window shopping. "I really shouldn't tell you. But I had to make a quiet trip up to the Shamir Diamond factory to set up some delivery schedules. I can't discuss those with anybody, even you. In the diamond business, you never can tell if someone is listening to you with a parabolic mike. It's like being a spy. So let's talk about something else." David felt strange spinning out a cover story. He probably sounded like an idiot. But he didn't have any choice. Over and above valuing his sense of honor, David didn't want to be shot.

Jasmine shrugged and acquiesced. What did it matter, anyway? The important thing was that her father was healing quickly, her mother was blissfully relieved, and she could get back to America, to Columbia, to normalcy! She wondered what had happened to Dr. Musawi.

Nobody at the hospital seemed to know, either. He had just disappeared one day with no notice. There was a rumor going around that he was a secret *jihadi*, that he had gone to Iraq or Afghanistan. She believed it. Their last conversation had been surreal.

They paused to look into a gift shop window, replete with silver candlesticks, bracelets, and similar items. Her first thought was that it was junk for the tourists. But it was really pretty. And tourists could have good taste too, couldn't they? She smiled. David could practically read her thoughts. He pulled her inside. "Come on, I think my girl needs a souvenir." She walked with him to a case containing ornately worked silver cuffs. The saleswoman, much less predatory than the harridans of 47th Street back home, walked over to help. David pointed to one with a repeating octagonal intaglio. The saleswoman unlocked the case and took it out. David slipped it around Jasmine's wrist. "It's beautiful, David, but I can't accept such an expensive gift. It wouldn't be right." David ignored her protestations. He pulled out his wallet and extracted an American Express card. American parents do not let their children go out into the wide world without a safety belt. He handed the card to the saleswoman, signed the little electronic tablet, and they were off.

Their El Al flight home was leaving at ten in the evening. Magically, David had been able to change his reservation so that they could travel together without paying a change fee. Equally miraculously, El Al had informed him that because of some overbooking problem, he and his companion would have to fly first class. Jasmine looked at David strangely while he made the changes over the phone, but he didn't say anything.

Privately he was thinking Boy! It's great to have friends in high places. Especially the highest places.

After retrieving Jasmine's suitcase from her hotel, they caught a cab to Sid and Nina Goldman's apartment. Jasmine waited on the curb with her luggage while David ran upstairs to pick up his. Nina gave David a quick hug. "We will miss you! I hope you will visit us again the next time you come to Israel. Travel safely!" Sid and David lugged the suitcase down the stairs and loaded both suitcases into Sid's jeep. Sid dropped David and Jasmine at the central bus station to catch the bus to Ben Gurion Airport.

August 15, 11:00 A.M . EDT   New York
School wouldn't start again for a week, so David once again was helping his *zayde* out. He was walking down 47th Street clutching a white paper bag full of cut diamonds. The sidewalk was full of pedestrians: midtown sharpies out for lunch, suburban shoppers, gawking tourists. Two big African-American men suddenly loomed up on the sidewalk in front of him, pushing an enormous hand truck loaded with cardboard boxes. David barely noticed. No dry mouth. No rising hair on the back of his neck. He waved to them. They waved back. David and the two men maneuvered around each other and kept going.

Things were different now,